APPEARANCES
and other stories

MARGO KRASNE

Wasteland Press

www.wastelandpress.net
Shelbyville, KY USA

Appearances and other stories
by Margo Krasne

First Printing – November 2012
ISBN: 978-1-60047-791-1
Front and back cover by Mark Berghash
Krasne photo by Michael Benabib

Printed in the U.S.A.

0   1   2   3   4   5   6   7   8   9   10

With love and gratitude to those who are gone.

Acknowledgements

First and foremost, thank you to my friends who put up with and supported me through the grueling but exhilarating process of storytelling. I am so grateful to all of you. I especially wish to acknowledge those friends who read the stories over and over as I wrote and rewrote line after line. So, to Dorothy Greenberg whose incessant "you can write!" kept me at it; Terry Gallo and Stephen Dolleck, Kimberly Birks, Hillary Megroz, Jill McBride and 'proofer extraordinaire' Loretta Sophocleous—thank you all!

To my editor Dave Gibbons–Wicki, thanks for the intro–Wow! While you list yourself simply as an editor, you are a fantastic teacher. I hope the final edition does you proud. To Mark Berghash, thank you for your work on the cover. You caught exactly what I wanted. And to Tim at Wasteland Publishing, thank you for putting up with all my questions and my desire to get it "just right."

Table of Contents

PART ONE

The Wallachs

The Bacher Boy

"You did go out with the Bacher boy, Alice, I remember it distinctly."

Alice looks at her mother propped up in bed—the stained rose-satin bed jacket in sharp contrast to her mother's alabaster skin now tinged with yellow violet veins–and tells a half-truth, "Well, I don't, Mom. I don't remember going out with him at all."

"But you did, dear. I'm certain of it."

"If you say so," Alice says as she rearranges the pillows. "There! Better?"

Alice needs to change the subject. The last thing she wants is to have old resentments creep in; she's worked too long and hard to put them at rest. Besides, this is not the time. Not the time at all.

"He was a nice young man, Alice."

"I'm sure he was, Mom."

"Very nice."

No use. Her mother's insistence pulls Alice back. . .

She wanted to fly to the door when the bell rang, having waited two whole weeks–more like one week and four days–for this moment to arrive. Two weeks since the young man had phoned, introducing himself as Steven, or Stephen, Alice wasn't sure which, saying he got her number from his mother, who got it from her mother, (meaning Alice's) and uh, well, did she want to go to a movie or something, maybe on Saturday? And although Alice was dying to say yes, she followed her mother's instructions and said she was sorry but she was busy this Saturday, however, the next one would be nice, if that was okay with him–breathing a huge sigh of relief when he said it was.

3

Alice refused to let it bother her that their fathers did business together. A piece of information picked up one evening at dinner when her mother asked her father what he thought of suggesting to Elsie Bacher their children get together and Alice's father answered, "Why the hell not? The *mamzer* owes me plenty!" causing Alice's mom to flinch and tell Alice not to mind. "Stevie Bacher goes to a good school, dear, and comes from a fine family" which left Alice to figure out how he could be the son of a *mamzer* and respectable at the same time. Not that she could tell what difference it made. She went to a good school and supposedly came from a fine family, and here she was, fifteen years old, and the Bacher boy would be her first real date, EVER!

Alice couldn't believe it was 8 o'clock and the bell had actually rung. Why just seconds ago she was staring at her untouched piece of three-layer strawberry cream cake, her very favorite dessert, asking to be excused "Puh-le-eeze," holding her breath as her father put down his fork, pushed back his chair, took out his pocket watch, winding it once as he always did, before proclaiming, "It's just 6:20. You've got plenty of time. Eat!"

Alice's eyes pleaded with her mom until she said, "Perhaps, dear, just this once?" procuring Alice permission to race to her room, throw off her shoes, socks, dress, and panties—her father forbidding robes and curlers worn to the table even on occasions as important as this—and get into clean undies, a padded bra, full-slip, her new garter belt and stockings, her pink angora sweater, and the new charcoal grey flared wool skirt, the pockets of which had been sewn together so Alice couldn't stick her hands in them and get them all out of shape. No, it was hard for Alice to believe the bell was finally ringing, because even though she'd gone through an incredible struggle to get her stocking seams straight, and four attempts to apply her pale pink lipstick without a smudge, smiling into the mirror the way she'd seen her mom do—Alice's mother applied a half-hour's worth of make-up each morning and another before Alice's father came home, yet somehow managing to look as if she wore none at all—it had taken Alice only eight minutes to get dressed, which left her approximately

4

ninety more with nothing to do. The longest ninety minutes she'd ever lived through.

She'd sat. Stood. Sat again. She called out to her mother "was he honestly, *honestly*" as tall as she was, "Cross your heart and hope to die." She even rang for the elevator to see if it was working. Not that she'd ever known it not to, except once when the elevator men went on strike. and she'd been allowed–with an adult in the car of course–to put her hand on the crank, pull it forward to go up and back to go down, thrilled, when sometimes on the very first try, she would manage to stop level to a floor. And she'd walked round and round their apartment at 81st Street and Central Park West, practicing just how she'd act when *he*–who was sure to be the image of Rhett Butler–walked through the door, whisked her off to the movies, and stared deep into her eyes over a chocolate ice cream soda, while her classmates drooled in envy.

Yes, Alice wanted to fly to the door when the bell rang, but stood instead in the doorway to her room listening to her mother's heels click along the black and gold linoleum squares in the foyer, her mother having insisted Alice stay put for a full five minutes after the young man arrived, so as not to appear eager. She heard the front door open, her mother's, "Why, Hello, Steven, do come in," the door close, and her mother suggest he take off his coat, explaining it would probably be some time before Alice came out. "But then you know all about young ladies and how it takes them forever to get ready, now don't you?" Then she heard her mother call and say, "Alice, dear. Steven's here. What on earth could be taking you so long?" Which is why Alice started down the hall to the foyer, only to be stopped short by her mother, her hand behind her back, signaling Alice to 'stay.' Still, she'd seen him. He hadn't seen her, but she had seen him. And his brown suit. And his hair–the exact color of a buff cocker spaniel's. And he *was* as tall as she was, exactly as promised. Unable to control herself, she peeked out again, but he was gone, her mother having escorted him into the living room out of view.

Alice watched the second hand of the hall clock go around two more times. Then, taking a deep breath, she walked into the foyer in the one-inch Cuban heels she'd convinced her mother to buy, her mother not having understood why in the world Alice would want to add insult to injury by making herself appear any taller than she already was. She'd practiced walking in her new shoes all week. Taking long strides on the linoleum. Letting her hips sway slightly, her pelvis tipped slightly forward–like the models she'd seen in magazines. What she hadn't done was practice on the white deep-piled living room rug, assuming they'd meet in the foyer. Another breath and with fingers crossed, she walked to the archway.

He was over on the far side of the room, by the baby grand piano, gazing intently at her mother. Alice didn't have to look at her mother. She already knew what she looked like, starting with the delicate feet easily balanced on the narrow, high-heeled, black suede shoes; the slender but shapely legs, with stocking seams that never wavered; the discrete but evident hips that narrowed to a minuscule waist; the grown-up breasts below the long elegant neck; and her face, with its painted lips, long straight nose, and pearl gray eyes. All of it leading to the silver strands of hair which wound around themselves and formed a knot on top of her mother's head, punctuating what had to be obvious to everyone—that all perfection ended here.

Alice's stomach let out a thunderous roar and she blurted out a loud, "Hi!"

"Why there she is," her mother said, and the young man looked over and said "Hi" back. Alice could only stare at his large brown eyes and slightly flushed cheeks.

"I was just showing Steven our family pictures, dear. Why don't you come over and join us?"

Alice smiled a tight-lipped smile to hide her braces and started to walk towards them as the young man returned to looking at the album. She got halfway across the room when her right foot crashed over on its side and she had to grab onto the back of her father's favorite chair to regain her balance.

"Now this one is of Alice's Aunt Bess, she died last year, and this is her Uncle Harry."

Alice bit her lip. The mere mention of Aunt Bess's name always causing her to well up. "And that's me, ages ago."

Alice could see the back of the young man's neck turn red and she knew they were looking at the picture of her mom voguishly posed, one hand behind her head, elbow to the sky, the other draped at her side, a towel dangling from her fingertips as if it were a feather boa.

Her mother looked up. "Alice, dear, why don't you go see what's keeping your father? Then you two can be on your way."

Alice didn't move.

"Go on, dear."

And Alice turned, carefully walking back across the living room as her mother inquired as to the young man's favorite subject. The very question Alice herself had planned to ask.

"Algebra," he said and Alice's stomach turned. She hated math.

"Why that's Alice's favorite, too," her mother said as Alice made it to the safety of the linoleum wondering what she was supposed to do if he asked her a formula or something.

"Damn it, Harry," her father said as she poked her head into the den. "I've told you time and time again we can't keep pouring money, hold on. . . What is it?"

"Mother, wants to know when you're coming out."

"Tell her, soon."

Alice waited.

"I mean it. Soon! Listen Harry. . ."

Alice walked back down the hall, through the foyer, once again stopping in the archway.

"Last, but never least," her mother was saying, and Alice knew they just had to have come to the photograph of Alice herself. The one in her gym uniform taken after her team won last year's basketball tournament. The young man seemed interested. It could almost be said he appeared eager. Oh, the knots in Alice's stomach began to dissolve, turning into butterflies, and she almost cried out for joy. Then she heard him say something about the debating team being the only team he'd ever been on, and her mother laughed, and

Alice wanted to die. How could she tell him she was terrible at sports? That she'd never made a basket, and the only reason she was even on the team was because of her height. He'd never believe her now.

Her mother went to close the book and somehow the button on the young man's jacket sleeve caught on her pearl bracelet, and her mother grabbed for the young man's arm and Alice's eyes filled with tears, her vision blurred, causing everything to change shape, and she saw the young man's ears grow long and floppy and fur sprout all over his face. . .

She couldn't believe her eyes. Neither could Alice's father, Bertram, or Bertram's brother, Harry, or Harry's wife, Alice's beloved Aunt Bess. Not one of the four standing in the foyer could believe what they were seeing. But there was Alice's mother, in the middle of the room and she was holding the puppy in her arms. Not simply in her arms, mind you, but close, really close, to her body. And she was pretending to be angry, and telling the puppy he was not allowed on the brand new carpeting and did he understand? Well, if he understood, he was the only one. Because only a short time earlier, Alice's mother had been telling Aunt Bess how she didn't relish having a dog in the house, any more than Alice's father did, but Alice, (God help them!) had simply worn them out with her pleading. "Why if it wasn't for that three-week trial period, well, let's just say whether we keep him or not will have all to do with how well Alice takes care of him. I hope you hear me, Alice, loud and clear." And Alice giggled, telling Aunt Bess how her mother jumped whenever a dog came near, and then she ran back to the window, for the umpteenth time, to look for her father's car coming up the block, and her mother told her to please calm down—in exactly the same tone she used whenever Alice's adored brother Rich came home from college and Alice followed him around the house begging him to dance with her–and Aunt Bess suggested she come sit next to her, and Uncle Harry went on about how you had to be mishuga to want a dog, "Mishuga! Who in their right mind wants to walk a dog!" But

Alice said she'd walk him, and feed him, and love him love him love him, no matter what, *forever*!

Finally, the key turned in the lock, the door opened, and there stood Alice's father with a light brown cocker spaniel under his arms. Aunt Bess said, "Oh, my, it's buff-colored." Alice's, mother, "Why so it is." And her father, "Fine. We'll call it Buffy!" ignoring Aunt Bess's, "What do you think, Alila?"

Alice rushed to give her Buffy a big welcoming hug as her father set him down and removed his leash. But the moment it came off, the puppy raced into the living room and Alice's mother, her fears for the new carpeting overcoming any she might have of puppies, scooped him up in her arms, and one of his ears caught on her pearl bracelet, and the pearls spilled all over the living room floor. Amazingly, she paid no attention. Not to the pearls or to the fact her black crepe dress, which never showed so much as the tiniest bit of lint, was now covered with buff colored hairs. She was talking in puppy talk, about how he was going to have to stay in her bathroom, and there'd be pretty newspaper on the floor, and as soon as he learned his manners, he'd be able to come out and join the family, so he should learn how to behave really soon, all right? Well, from that moment on, the puppy loved Alice's mother, and only Alice's mother, following her everywhere like Mary and her little lamb.

No matter, Alice walked him. Before and after school. Every single day for the first week, although it did embarrass her to stand there while he did "his thing." When he finished, she would bring him home, take off his leash, and watch as he raced to her mother for a pat on the head for having done his thing so well.

Alice spent hours next to her Buffy on the floor of her mother's bathroom–feeling the cold of the black and white tiles through the carefully laid newspaper. She'd tell him anything and everything she thought might be of interest. Like how her mother tried to get her father to replace the pearls with a gold bracelet, but her father had said she should get them restrung, one new piece of jewelry a year is more than enough. And how Aunt Bess and Uncle Harry were driving to Florida for two weeks, which her father thought was crazy, as this was 1948 and you could now fly, or take a train, like normal people. And she would tell the puppy how much she loved him, putting her nose to his and rubbing his belly.

Sometimes his large almond shaped eyes looked lovingly at her, and his long droopy ears would rise at their tops, and Alice would feel she was bursting. But if he heard her mother's voice on the other side of the door, or even—Alice was convinced–her breathing, his tail would wag, and he'd race to the bathroom door, scratching at it until his real mistress came to let him out.

The second week Alice decided if the puppy so preferred her mother, her mother could walk him. Of course, her mother thought the idea ridiculous. It was, after all, Alice's dog. So, Alice's father, who had never, not ever, been seen in public without being clean shaven and perfectly groomed, put his pants on over his pajamas, his coat on over his pants, and, at seven in the morning, without even a sip of coffee, took the dog out for his walk as Alice watched from her window.

Then, Alice, who had been feeding the puppy three times a day as directed, refused to feed him any longer, mumbling if he so preferred her mother, her mother could feed him. And Anna, the cook, who could not understand why a puppy had to be fed certain foods at certain times, fed him whenever he begged, and the puppy's belly became big and fat, until it dragged along the floor, and he got very, very sick. On the day before the three-week trial period was up, the puppy was returned to the kennel. Alice didn't go to school. She got cramps and stayed in bed for days. . .

Alice stood in the living room hearing her mother reassure the young man how it wasn't his fault they collided. Why he could see for himself no damage had been done. And Alice mumbled something about if the young man so preferred her mother, her mother should go out with him. But her mother didn't hear her. Neither did the young man.

"I'm not feeling well, Mother," Alice mumbled.

"What?"

"I said, I'm not feeling well."

"Alice, I'm sure it's nothing. As soon as you and Steven are on your way, you'll be just fine."

"No, I won't. I need to stay home. Good night, Steven. I'm sorry." With that she turned and left the room. She didn't have to look at her mother to know her lips had tightened and her eyes were flashing fury. But she didn't care. Her mother would apologize. Probably even offer Steven a coke or a piece of the strawberry cake. . .

"Well, I know you went out with the Bacher boy."

Alice shrugs

"I even remember what movie you saw. Oh what was the name, you used to sing all the songs. Something about a wedding."

"Next you'll tell me you remember it starred Fred Astaire and Jane Powell."

"See you do remember."

"For God's sake, Mom, we all saw that film, at least a million times."

"But you didn't tell him you'd already seen it."

"How do you remember that?"

"Well, it wasn't as if you had that many dates, dear. . . They say he married well."

"Good for him."

"You know, Alice, we tried to introduce you to some very nice young men. You just never were that interested. Well, at least I made sure you looked nice. Especially that night. I can still see you all dressed up in your pretty white blouse."

"It was a pink angora sweater."

"I thought you couldn't remember."

"I can remember getting ready, Mom. Just not going."

"That's silly."

Not silly. Not the run to her room as her braces punctured her lips. Nor her fury as she slammed the door, kicked off her shoes, unzipped the gray flannel pleated skirt, tossing it on the chair along with the pink angora sweater that was sure to shed–her rage barely contained as she flung the padded bra and slip on the pile, ignoring that they missed their target and landed on the floor. Not silly her tears as she wrapped herself in the ratty maroon bathrobe–the one she refused to let her mother give away—and plopped down on the bed cross-legged, to make sure her knees burst through the new stockings before turning up the radio really loud.

Alice runs a comb through her mom's hair. She does have a vague recollection of sitting in a movie theater next to a young man with a camel's hair coat folded neatly on his lap, hers kept on disliking the awkwardness of taking it off. It could have been the Bacher boy, perhaps on another night. Or not.

The Move

It was a time when upper middle class Jewish "mercantiles" lined Central Park West from Ninety-Second Street down to the low sixties. When a number of families such as hers–no, not such as hers, when *her* family chose to abandon the only home Alice had known: a sprawling apartment, with magnificent views that overlooked the reservoir. Where, curled up on one of the two inside window ledges of her room, she could lose herself for hours watching other children climb the endless variety of rocks in summer and belly-flop down snow-covered hills in winter. She would sit spellbound as the well-groomed horses, with their stylishly decked out riders, moved at varying gaits around the bridal path. And she was awed by the incredible array of trees–one white dogwood in particular that annually popped its buds a month too early. A home her family would relinquish–on the very day of her sixteenth birthday no less— moving across the park to a far smaller apartment, in the back of a building, where her only view would be other people's curtained windows. The reason proffered: her safety!

For, you see, it was also a time when the first waves of Puerto Ricans descended onto the side streets of the upper West Side, cramming single rooms of once privately owned brownstones with entire families. The men, in undershirts, played their bongos on the stoops and roofs; their women, bosoms and buttocks clearly delineated beneath unseemly outfits, moved provocatively with or without music. Adults, on the stoops, drank from bottles in paper bags. And the children, seemingly hundreds of them, darted between parked cars and out into the street, causing cursing drivers to slam on their brakes, only to be met with rapid-fire outbursts that bore no resemblance to the Spanish Alice was learning in school. The spectacle did not abate when winter's cold drove the intruders indoors; the climate-induced confinement ratcheting up what could only be labeled as highly inappropriate displays of emotion, inducing discordant sounds to build up, until they exploded through the closed windows, shattering the silence of a once sedate neighborhood.

Just as one keeps an ear for passing sirens, for well over a year the Wallach family had kept theirs tuned to the on-going dramas below. If the racket escalated, or stopped suddenly, Alice and her parents would race to a side window and stare agape at heretofore unseen sights: a man slamming a woman against a car, two women clawing at each other, a man throwing another to the sidewalk. One time, a knife-wielding male chased a female all the way down the block to Columbus Avenue where they disappeared around the corner, only to reappear some time later with the female, knife now in hand, chasing the male. It was all Alice's parents could talk about.

And talk they did. Between themselves. In front of Alice. Even in front of the help–though in lowered voices. They talked over cards at their rotating Tuesday and Thursday night games. They talked through their special Saturday night dinner parties: lavish affairs begun in the den with cocktails, platters of shrimp, sometimes caviar, always smoked salmon, garnished with radishes carved to look like roses, and the ever present sterling silver bread basket filled with crackers and toasted bagels. They talked as they ambled through the massive foyer into the dining room, finding their place cards, their names written in Alice's mother's exquisite script, seating themselves around the extended table draped in a damask cloth, the centerpiece, a green and white porcelain fruit-filled bowl, placed between two three-armed candelabras, their candles dripping wax. And they talked in between toasts made with champagne in the crystal etched Baccarat glasses, after they dug into the crabmeat and avocado appetizer arranged in gilded goblets, and after they chewed and swallowed slices of the succulent roast. "Who lives that way, just tell me? Who, I ask you? Dreck, that's who!" If Alice's father remembered the over-crowded tenements he and his family inhabited when they first came to this country, he never let on. At the proper time he would take the cue from his wife, stick his fingers into the crystal finger bowl, wipe them on his napkin, finding room for the cook's special apple-crisps and coffee before enjoining his guests to adjourn–women to the living room, men to the den–for an evening of Canasta and Gin, respectively.

Most of the Wallachs' friends could be divided into two groups comprised of four couples each. (Five the preferred number for an evening of cards, as it allowed each person a time out without impeding the flow of a game.) In the aggregate, the combined incomes of each group didn't vary much. Yet they did not mix well. It had to do with style. One group had it; the other didn't. It was with the latter group–"the B's," as Alice called them–with whom her parents appeared more at ease. However, it was the A's—already ensconced on the East Side, though only one with a Fifth Avenue address–to which they aspired. "No need for so many rooms," Alice's parents would say before asking for a list of the better buildings, which ones took Jews, and what it would take to assure board approval. "A smaller place just makes sense, what with Helen and Rich married and Alice going to college in a year or so." Left unsaid: "We need an affordable address but one respectable enough from which to marry Alice off." This even though Alice had already announced she had no intention of getting married until she turned at least thirty-two, a number arrived at one morning by doubling her upcoming birthday, as she lay in bed turning the reflections of the sun's rays on her pink walls into various figures, faces and whole canvasses of scenery. The evenings always ended with Alice's parents reminding the A's to let them know the minute they heard of an opening—"perhaps where you live?"

It was different with the B's. With them, Alice's parents discussed whether to rent or buy, implying they could do either. They didn't mention they were looking for a better building, as one of the B couples–a newspaper man and his wife–lived in Queens where Alice's father refused to go, even for a card game. Queens a place you passed through on your way to the beach in the summer, just as you only went to the Bronx for business, even though Alice's mother's brother lived with his family on the Grand Concourse.

Alice consoled herself that it was only talk, that an actual move would never occur. Then, one Thursday, a few weeks before Christmas vacation and Alice's impending birthday, as she descended from the school bus in front of her building, a boy no more than sixteen or seventeen and obviously from one of the buildings around the corner, rode his bike onto the sidewalk, aimed it straight at Alice and proceeded to make vulgar sounds through thick pursed lips. Only when he'd come within inches of her tall gangly frame did he swerve away and ride off, laughing. She wanted to yell at him. To show the boys on the school bus, who might still be watching, she could stand up to a bully. But nothing came out of her mouth. Just as nothing had when Max Teitle beat her up and her mother had called the school to complain, making Alice's life even worse than before. Nothing came out of the doorman's mouth either. Nor a neighbor's leaving the building. So Alice promised herself she wouldn't say a word either, but when she opened the front door and saw her mother in the foyer, out it came, in one large blurt. Of course, her mother repeated the story to Alice's father, adding a bit more here and there, until it sounded as if Alice had been physically assaulted. If her father had looked up, he would have seen she was fine. But he didn't. "Enough!" he said. "We're moving!" And Alice wanted to kick herself for not keeping her mouth shut.

If there were a possibility that her father would change his mind, it was extinguished that evening at cards, when one of the wealthiest "A" men, the one with a Fifth Avenue address, said, "I must tell you, Bert, for the last few months I've been uncomfortable coming over here. And now with what happened to Alice. . . well, it's going to make me think twice. . ." making the Upper West Side sound like another undesirable borough.

That did it! For the next two weekends Alice was forced to traipse with her parents, from apartment to apartment, on the other side of the park. She hated all of them. They were dark and small. When Alice asked why they couldn't look at nicer places, her mother gave her a look of derision. "Don't be childish," she said. "We're not millionaires, you know," which made no sense to Alice, as her parents certainly made it appear they were, except at restaurants, where her mother always whispered to check the right side of the menu before considering what to eat. A habit Alice would never be able to break, even when others were treating.

By the end of the two weeks a decision was made. It would not be any of the apartments they'd seen, but one which, unbeknownst to Alice, had been offered them weeks before. One that required they take whatever monies they had, borrow a bit more from an uncle who was a real millionaire, and buy their first piece of property ever: the smaller apartment, without a view of the park, in a building fronted by a grey awning, with white lettering that spelled "Fifth Avenue," even though the entrance was actually on a side street.

There was one problem, though. One her parents spent the next few weeks trying to solve, even after the deed had been signed, a moving date set, a mover found, and the decorator sent in search of fabrics to update the furniture. The new apartment had only two bedrooms. (Not counting the two maid's rooms, of course.) This meant Alice's father would have to relinquish his cherished den—a room converted from the bedroom Alice's sister's left empty when she married and, once the war was over, a room transformed into a luxurious setting for Mr. Wallach's cocktail hour and weekly card games. A cocoon, with deep blood-red walls, red carpeting, red sofa, red leather-top card table with matching red leather chairs, and two red-stained floor-to-ceiling bookshelves–one of which housed a bar and the other a desk. These contained the only books to be found at the Wallachs (not including Alice's): a complete set of leather-bound Dickens, all eleven volumes of The Book of Knowledge, and the Passover Haggadahs, along with some of the latest bestsellers. The Red Room they called it. Her father's refuge. One that nightly affirmed his place in the world and a loss as devastating for him as the loss of the park was for Alice.

Still, as her mother liked to say, where there's a will. . . so with great ingenuity a solution was found. On the two or three nights a week they entertained, their daughter would stay in one of the two maid's rooms off the kitchen—the live-in cook Anna residing in the other. The rest of the time the den would be hers, as long as she kept it visibly free of personal items. Yes, the maid's room was far away from any bathroom—the one between the rooms closed off so Anna could have her privacy—and yes, a small part of the 10-by-6 foot space would be needed for storage, but the decorator assured them it would be doable.

When Alice's face turned to stone at the thought of it, her mother admonished, "Just tell me how many children have two rooms they could show off?"—ignoring how hard it would be for Alice to study with the cook and waitresses yelling at each other in their Slavic languages, the platters clanking, and the laughter from the guests crashing in unexpected spurts through the door. No choice, according to her parents. It would take too long to clear the dishes and ready the dining room for the men, nor could they be relegated to the sixteen-by-twelve foot foyer what with the women so close by. There were cigars to be smoked, and man-talk to be made. "Besides, it's only for twenty-one months and then you'll be off to college, for heaven's sake."

A week before the move, Alice accompanied her mother to the new apartment. "Go, look at your new room," her mother said, pointing towards the kitchen. "See how nice it turned out." It hadn't. The room, which looked small when empty, now seemed even smaller. On the right of the door, a cabinet, which housed the dining table leaves, along with an extra folding card table, did double duty as a headboard for the narrow bed covered in a purple-weave fabric; on the left, a shallow closet for canned goods and liquor. The desk, a long purple shiny Formica slab, ran from the cabinet to the window facing the courtyard. A plastic lamp hung over the desk and a few shelves on metal hinges were set above for her books. Alice found it hard to breathe—momentary claustrophobia propelling her back into the foyer to look for her mother.

She wasn't to be found in either the dining or living rooms, so Alice headed towards the bedrooms. There she was, in Alice's other room, on her hands and knees, rolling out large sheets of paper on the newly stained floors. Alice was stunned. Her mother looked like one of those perfect 1950's TV moms who made breakfast, did the laundry, cleaned up after the family. Not that Alice's mother was in a cotton house dress and bandana or anything of the sort. No, she was impeccably garbed in an outfit a TV Mom would have worn to dinner at the home of her husband's boss: A dark blue shantung dress, pearls around her neck. Only her shoes were off, left at the door. Alice had never, ever, seen her mother do anything physical. It was Anna the cook who prepared the meals and Tessie—Alice's caretaker and the Wallach's maid, waitress, seamstress and laundress wrapped into one—who labored. Alice stood transfixed. The sight before her so incongruous and yet so perfect.

Then, just as she opened her mouth to tell her mom how beautiful she looked, her mother turned, saw Alice smiling, and flew into a rage. "What kind of a daughter stands there watching her mother pick papers up and doesn't rush to help? You like seeing me as a maid? Is that why you're smiling?" Alice couldn't find her voice. Yes, her mom could get upset, turn red, and cry. And yes, she could be dismissive. But rage? This was new. Alice froze. Her mother rose up, slammed into her shoes, stormed to the foyer, grabbed her coat, and demanded Alice follow. Alice couldn't speak, her jumbled thoughts blocking her words. It made for an excruciatingly silent trip back across the park.

Once home, Alice's mother took to her bed and the phone, immediately calling her other daughter Helen. Alice took to her window trying to block out her mother's tearful complaints audible through the wall. She knew exactly what would follow: when her father came home, her mother would recount the events; he would become furious with Alice and refuse to acknowledge her existence; life would be more or less hell; then she'd apologize. By the time the apology took place, she and her father rarely remembered what caused her original expulsion from the world of the living. This time Alice decided not to wait. It was too close to her birthday.

"Mom," Alice said, sinking to the floor next to her mother's bed. "I'm sorry. Really! I didn't mean anything wrong." "I just don't understand you, Alice," her mother's reply. And Alice continued to beg her mother not to be upset, and her mother cried, causing Alice to well up, a reflexive reaction she could never control, though this time it made her apology sound much more heartfelt than it actually was. "All right then," her mother said, gaining control over her emotions. "But no sweet sixteen birthday party. That's cancelled!"

Alice wanted to ask what one thing had to do with another, but didn't. All she could think about was facing her disinvited classmates. She needn't have worried. When she did bring it up, none of them knew what she was talking about. Still, she thought, maybe if not a party, there would be something to commemorate her coming of age. But no, on the day of her birthday, after the movers had packed up the final truck, she and her parents got into a cab, drove through the transverse to their new address, and spent the rest of the day unpacking.

This is not to say that Alice didn't receive an amazing gift. She did--three weeks later on a Wednesday, at 7:15 in the morning when the door to her room opened and her mother entered, fully clothed, carrying a breakfast tray. It wasn't that Alice's mother hadn't been getting up and dressed every morning since the move. She had. To greet the painters, plumbers and any other workers hired by the decorator. But carrying a tray–and for Alice? Her breakfast was normally in the dining room prepared by the cook; her parents' by her father who brewed the coffee, heated the rolls, then set everything out on the two trays the cook had laid out the night before. The trays then carried into the bedroom where her mother waited in bed, the sheet pulled up over her, ready to discuss that night's meal. The ritual had gone on as long as Alice could remember. But on this morning there was her mom, tray in hand.

"I don't want you getting upset dear, but the police are here and I don't want you going into the kitchen," her mother said, setting down the tray.

"The police?" Alice gasped, "Why?"

"There's a woman outside our back door. Dead. A maid from one of the upper floors."

"You're kidding!" Alice said.

"I wouldn't kid about something like that, Alice. Now please eat your breakfast. I don't want you late for the bus."

Alice couldn't contain herself. A body right outside their door? Nothing like that had ever happened on the West Side. She could kick herself for not having slept in the room off the kitchen. She'd have gotten so many more details. Of course, she felt for the poor woman, but it made such a great story. Alice told it the minute she got on the bus, reveling in her new found fame. Of course, there was a strong possibility that her bus mates thought her a bit weird as she kept breaking into giggles with each telling to each new arrival. The questions kept coming throughout the day: had she seen the body; was it murder or suicide; did they know who did it? Alice said she'd find out the details and report back the next day. But when she got home, it was as if it never happened. Her parents refused to talk about it and all Anna would say was the painters had found the poor thing with a kitchen knife in her chest.

Alice tried to imagine what drove the woman to take her own life, if that's what she did. There certainly had been plenty of times Alice had contemplated doing the same thing, her fantasies stalled as she fixated on her father's eulogy for his daughter. Would it be one of loss, or fury over her having caused her parents needless distress? He certainly blamed her now for the loss of his beloved den. How many times in the last few weeks had he come into her room at cocktail hour, drink in hand, trying to make conversation, then leave as he realized (for the moment) the room was no longer his?

Alice decided murder would be far more interesting than suicide. No one would know the difference. It would never hit the newspapers what with the woman being only a maid. Besides, who would thrust a knife into herself except maybe Madame Butterfly? And Alice was certain she'd never seen a Japanese maid in the building. Come to think of it, Alice couldn't remember ever seeing a Japanese person anywhere except in the newsreels. No, if it were suicide, the woman would have found another way. Poison. A razor blade. Not a knife. So, when a few weeks later her English teacher, Miss Fanelli, asked the class to write about something they, or their family, had experienced, Alice knew which story to tell. It would start: "The uphill trek that began for him in a mud-flat shtetl outside Odessa, and for her at the turn of the century in Harlem–the climb that took them both from the Bronx to West End Avenue to Central Park West–ended on Fifth Avenue in a pool of blood." She'd call it "We've Arrived!"

In The Living Room

"That!" Alice's father's voice fills the room, just as his thin five foot eight inch frame manages to fill the large red cushioned chair he claims as his own. "That!" he repeats "is what a young woman is supposed to look like!" He looks around to make sure all eyes follow his hand– holding the heavy crystal glass, filled with two jiggers of scotch over one piece of ice–as it sweeps in Evelyn's direction. His eyes radiate pleasure. He sure knows a looker when he sees one.

The object of his admiration exhibits none of the disdain she will later express when she calls him a letch. Right now all that appears is the studied smile often found curling around the lips of her alabaster face. But then she is a model. Has been one since she was fifteen. She knows how to strike a pose.

"And her posture," he continues. "Look at it! Perfect."

Why shouldn't it be? She is also a Four-Star General's daughter.

On the other side of the room, on opposite ends of the celadon green silk sofa, beneath a portrait of a woman draped with Greco-Roman artifice, sit Alice's mother and sister Helen–scotch and waters in hand, elbows on the sofa's arms, their legs crossed towards each other. Both women a picture in Mollie Parnis black–their almost matching, silk shantung full-skirted dresses with accompanying jackets, discretely cover décolletage and knees, respectively.

Tessie, thin, skinny, overworked Tessie, is in waitress garb. Not shantung, of course, but shiny black polyester cotton. She also has on a white apron, and even a small white laced cap on her head. Her pale cracked hands hold a tray of hors d'oeuvres–bite-sized pieces of sharp cheddar smothered with butter, rolled in crust-less pieces of white bread, and grilled. "Cheese things" the Wallach's call them. They are a favorite of Alice's father. Alice's too, for that matter.

Evelyn sits in the small antique curved chair set catty-corner into the room facing Mr. Wallach, her sherry glass held gracefully between her thumb and third finger, pinky extended. She's in a body fitting black jersey dress, with a scooped neckline, and long sleeves to the wrist, the hem of her dress–a discrete inch above her knees–frames her thin, pale, nylon clad legs. Her high-heeled, low-cut, size five, black suede pumps show off the delicate feet. Her only piece of jewelry: a thin silver chain with a miniature diamond heart.

Completing the scene, off to the side, is Alice, scrunched on the love seat, in a pair of black leotard and tights, one of a number she wears daily underneath her black jersey skirt with its elastic waistband. Her flat brown loafers lie empty on the plush white carpeting. Her legs curled up beneath her skirt. In her hand a coke.

"Well, am I right?" Mr. Wallach asks of no one in particular, his eyes bright with excitement.

Evelyn responds. "That's very sweet, Mr. Wallach," If you listen carefully you can catch the tinges of disdain in her voice. It's those tinges that make Evelyn so attractive to so many. Her ability to remain aloof. Cool if not outright cold.

The ice in Mr. Wallach's glass clinks as he sweeps his hand towards Alice. "Why can't you dress like that?" he says. His eyes hold their delight, his mouth its smile. It's his voice that has lost the tease.

"Dear!" Mrs. Wallach admonishes softly as if their company can't hear, "Please."

Alice draws her skirt tighter over her legs.

"Shmatas. Black shmatas she wears," his Russian shtetl accent discernible.

Alice's mom signals with her eyes for Tessie to bring the tray to Mr. Wallach. He starts to wave Tessie away, changes his mind and motions her back. "Don't tell me anyone in that school you two go to dresses like her," then he pops another cheese thing into his mouth.

Alice expects Evelyn to say, yes, we all do, which would not be entirely true, but close enough. Instead, Evelyn says, "I changed before I came here, Mr. Wallach."

"From what?" Mr. Wallach asks. "Nothing like what she's wearing, I bet." He takes another sip of scotch as if it's his reward. "And makeup!" he says, you wear makeup. She can't even put on lipstick."

"I am wearing makeup," Alice mumbles.

"What?" Alice's father says. "I can't hear you."

"I am wearing makeup," Alice repeats with a bit more volume.

"Black shmutz around the eyes is makeup?"

Tessie is now standing directly in front of Alice silently pleading for her to eat something. Poor Tessie. She's impotent to do battle in Alice's defense.

Alice is one of Tessie's surrogate children. Tessie had a boy once. Jimmy Brenner. She cared for him until his family no longer needed her and the Wallachs did. Then she went to work for them as their maid, laundress, seamstress, waitress, as well as Alice's babysitter and playmate. Tessie still talks about Jimmy, but Alice is no longer jealous. She shakes her head 'no' to Tessie's offering and Tessie, trying to smile, moves on. Even when Tessie smiles it appears as if she's crying.

Alice prays her sister will get her father to change subjects. Mr. Wallach worships Helen, and usually does whatever she says. But tonight her sister stays mute. Alice doesn't look to her mother for help. Alice already knows her mother is thinking, "I told you to change when you came home," and the reason she hadn't was she expected Evelyn to come directly from school, dressed in her usual skirt, sweater and flats. Besides, Evelyn was a friend, not company.

Mr. Wallach continues his harangue and Alice tries hard not to listen. But her eyes well up distorting the woman in the painting, and the two on the sofa, until they appear as shapes seen through a windshield in a rainstorm. Alice digs the nail of her third finger into her thumb. It's a trick her father taught her. Inflict pain on one part of your body to keep your feelings from showing. Only it doesn't work. Well, she will not break down in front of him. Not!

Alice uncurls her legs, shoves her size nine feet into her shoes, and rises from the love seat. She turns her back on her father, her face from the women on the sofa and walks past Evelyn in her chair, not even giving her a nod of recognition. She passes Tessie—now in the foyer and at a loss as to which way to turn—and heads down the hall to the bathroom. The guest bathroom. Her bathroom, even though none of her personal items are ever to remain in view.

Her father's voice follows her. "I'm trying to have a discussion," he yells. "But no, she has to run away. So go! Slam the door while you're at it. Gevalt."

Alice quietly closes the door and locks it, all the while pressing a hand over her mouth. It doesn't help. The sob she's been holding in belches up full force. It echoes along the pink tiles of the bathroom she painted under her parents' decorator's direction— blue, white and black striated lines meant to imitate marble. Why had she invited Evelyn anyway? To show her off? To prove to her father that she, Alice, had friends of caliber? What difference? Evelyn: a thousand. Alice: zero.

There's a tentative tapping on the bathroom door. Alice knows its Tessie. Tessie can run on concrete and not make a sound.

"Alice? Alice? You okay?" Tessie whispers.

Alice can't answer.

"Alice, please come out."

Alice chokes past the sob blocking her throat. "Can't. . .Leave me alone, Tess. . . Please. . . Please, go away."

And Tessie does. She is used to taking orders.

Alice stares into the mirror. The tears continue to contort her face. Her eyes red and bulging. She used to look in the mirror and her eyes would smile back. Her father liked her eyes. "Fix your nose and those eyes would show," he'd say. Obviously the nose job hadn't helped.

She opens the medicine cabinet over the sink: Peroxide, talc, her brush, black eye-liner, Tampax, a razor, blades. She tries to imagine going back to school. No way she could. They'll all talk. Evelyn will make sure of that. Tell them how crazy Alice is. How emotional. It had happened before. Not with Evelyn, but eight years or so ago when Susie Bernstein came for a sleep-over–Alice's very first. Her parents were out; Tessie had gone home, leaving Susie, and Alice basically alone–Anna, the cook being in her room behind the kitchen out of earshot. Susie demanded a pillow fight, saying it wasn't a sleepover unless you had one. So Alice picked up a pillow, tossed it and Susie tossed it back. Then, a pillow in hand, Susie began hitting Alice who dreaded conflict of any kind. Her usual response either to freeze or flee. But as the perfect host, she was required to continue, even as her emotions overwhelmed and she began to panic. So she picked up a pillow and hit back. At one point, her fear rose emerging as a scream, but if she actually said anything, she couldn't be sure. Suddenly Susie stopped playing and opened up her pink, round overnight case, took off her PJs, and began to pack. Alice panicked. "What are you doing?" she cried. And Susie said, "You threw me out." And Alice said, "No, I didn't. I didn't." And Susie said, "Yes, you did," and then she took her coat from the hall closet and walked to the elevator with Alice running after her, begging she stay, all the while knowing that her parents would be furious if they came home and found Susie gone. Then, just as the elevator arrived, Susie, a smirk on her face, turned, marched back into Alice's room, put on her PJ's and went to bed. No explanation, no nothing. An hour later, when Alice's mother poked her head into the room to check on them, Alice pretended to be asleep. But it didn't end there. The next day at school Susan told everyone Alice had kicked her out. And they all believed her. As did Alice's parents, when Susan's mother called demanding to know what kind of daughter they had.

Alice takes a razor blade out of the packet. She's had enough. Nothing will change. She has no more energy left to do battle. The new blade is sharp. She is familiar with razor cuts. Every time she shaves her legs or under her arms she draws blood. Better that then letting her father render her a cut-free shave as he continually wants to do. Once had been more than enough.

Another unexpected sob swells up; only the sound it makes is matched in intensity by a loud voice–the words indecipherable. She thinks it's Helen's, but that doesn't make sense. Helen never has to raise her voice to be heard. Alice places the blade on the edge of the sink, flicks off the switch so no light will show, and ever so quietly cracks open the door. It is her sister. "How could you, Dad? How could you?" she's saying. Alice has never heard Helen talk back to their father. Never heard her so emotional ever. The one time Alice told her sister she loved her, Helen responded, "don't be so dramatic" and left the room. And now it was she who was spewing forth. "And you Evelyn, I think you better leave. Now!"

Alice hears shoes click on the linoleum floor of the foyer. She quickly steps back into the dark bathroom, and pulls the door until it is almost closed. "Your coat, Evelyn" Helen says. Alice can't hear Evelyn's response only the front door opening and closing, then momentary silence followed by an explosion of words each one reaching inside Alice as none had before. "She's a porcelain doll, Dad? An empty porcelain doll! Alice has depth for God's sake! Can't you see that? What is wrong with you, Dad? What the hell is wrong with you?"

Alice is stunned. Yes, whenever their parents were away, her sister was on call. But Alice assumed that like everyone else in the family, her sister acted out of duty. And yes, it was Helen who explained menstruation and masturbation and most things sexual. And it was her sister who came to Alice's high school graduation with their mother, but Alice had figured her mother required company, not that her sister actually cared.

Tessie's voice startles Alice. "Dinner is served," she whispers. "Please come and eat."

"Soon," Alice says and closes the door. She replaces the blade in the cabinet, tosses cold water on her face and reapplies heavy black liner to her eyes. She takes her brush from the cabinet, runs it through her hair and leaves it out on the sink. She's got depth, does she? Well, well, well. And with that she leaves the bathroom and goes down the hall to dinner.

Truce

They had been at war since she was six months old. A war, according to her mother, Alice had started. "I know you were six months. Six months! We just couldn't understand it."

Well, neither could Alice. But she'd accepted her mother's version, the way, as a child, she used to accept their cook Anna's servings of liver and spinach. No matter how she tried to keep her mouth closed, eventually her lips would part and she'd swallow every bite. Well, no more. Not to render metaphorical overkill, but digesting what her mom had been dishing out was over. The time for a refutation had come. Besides, she was under express orders to "Do it!"

"Mom, you have to think it strange I was capable of hating anyone, nevertheless my own father, at six months of age?" She knows the response will be borne, as always, on a sigh of resignation. It is.

"I'm not saying it wasn't strange, just that's the way it was."

"You've got to realize how crazy that sounds."

"Oh, Alice, please. This is neither the time nor the place."

Stuck behind a garbage truck, with the cab's meter ticking away, seemed as good a time and place as any. "Humor me, Mom. Repeat the whole story one more time." There was always the chance of some new twist throwing light on what had actually happened.

"Don't be childish, Alice."

And Alice whines, "Mo-om, it's important" more than validating the 'childish' label.

"It's that therapist of yours provoking you, isn't it?" her mother accurately determines. It fascinates Alice how mothers can do this, not being one herself. Still, she lies, "I'm doing this all on my own."

"You can tell your therapist when you were six months old, your father brought Dave Karp into your room and. . ."

"I thought it was Sam Bacher."

"Sam, Dave. What difference?"

"For one thing, if you don't have that part of the story right, the rest might not be right either." Ha!

"For heaven's sake, Alice. I can't be expected to remember everything. Besides," her voice falling to a whisper, "it was over thirty years ago."

And Alice says, loud enough so the driver will hear, "Thirty-five to be exact." Without looking she knows that by broadcasting her age, she has caused her mom's eyebrows to raise, and her jaw to droop just enough, so her appearance is now one of a martyred saint in a fourteenth century icon–quite a feat for a New York Jewish woman.

The driver, finding an opening in the traffic, lurches forward, throwing both women back against their seats. "Maybe I wasn't in your room when it happened," the veins in her neck bulge against her white skin as she grips the strap, "but I was certainly in the house. Driver, could you slow down just a bit, please."

Alice also wishes the driver would slow down, but for another reason entirely. "In other words, you don't actually know what took place, do you, Mom?"

"It was more than obvious what happened, Alice. My God! Why else would Sam, Dave, whoever, come out and say, 'Hey, Bert, I guess your daughter doesn't like you?' Why else if it weren't so apparent you didn't?" Clearly her mother wasn't giving up either.

"Sam or Dave could have been kidding, Mom."

"People don't kid about things like that, Alice. Your father brought him into your room to show you off. And what do you do? You start screaming. Oh, Alice, you can't blame your father for staying away from you from that point on. You just can't. My God! You know how sensitive he is."

"Hey, Lady!" the cabdriver's gravelly voice booms back across the divider. "That's nuts. That's really nuts. A six month old kid screams and your husband takes it personally? Is he crazy or somethin'?"

Her mother turns pale. Alabaster pale. Worrisome pale. Maybe, Alice worries, she went too far. Maybe this isn't the time.

"Listen, Lady," he continues. "Maybe she'd a pin stickin' in her. Or maybe the kid pissed or somethin'."

Alice can't help herself. "You'd be exactly right, except both my parents swear there was no pin, no wetness, nor. . ."

"Alice!" Her mother pleads.

"Okay," The driver says. "So she wasn't wet. So maybe she was havin' a lousy dream."

Alice can't believe what she's hearing. A total stranger, a cab driver yet!–not that cab drivers can't be insightful–got in a few blocks what took her three years of therapy to grasp. So what if he's talking about her as if she's not sitting right behind him, something that normally has her climbing walls. He is saying exactly what she wants her mother to hear. She leans over to get his name. Steiner.

"Mr. Steiner, that's exactly what I've been trying to explain to my mother. There could have been all sorts of reasons why I cried."

"Sure. Listen, Lady. Maybe your husband had a cigar. My grandchild? She hates my cigar. Yells something awful if I come in with it."

"See, Mom," she says. "And I'm sure Mr. Steiner's grandchild doesn't hate him. Does she, Mr. Steiner?"

"Alice, will you please stop!" a bit of color creeping back into her face. "Now listen to me. You are well aware your father never smoked a day in his life."

"But maybe Sam or Dave did. I seem to remember Dave Karp with a large cigar stuck in his mouth."

"Sure makes sense to me," Mr. Steiner chimes in.

"Driver," her mother's tone of voice letting him know he'd overstepped his bounds. "If you don't mind, this is between my daughter and me."

"All what I'm tellin' you, Lady, is there's lots of reasons a kid cries. Maybe your husband was makin' a noise. Or maybe he smelled. Does your husband like pastrami? So maybe he had pastrami for lunch."

Alice can't help herself. She starts to giggle.

"You had to start this, Alice, didn't you?" her Mom hisses. "There's no earthly reason we should be going into all of this again. Especially now!"

"Sorry." It's obvious she's anything but.

"So who's in the hospital, Lady? Your husband?"

Her mother doesn't answer. Her head turned again towards the window. Alice answers for her. "Yes."

"Too bad. What's he got?"

"Old age. And a growth in his esophagus," which prompts:

"The world doesn't have to know our business, Alice."

But, for Alice, Mr. Steiner isn't the world. He's the man who has come up with more reasons than Alice's therapist as to why she screamed. No, Mr. Steiner is her ally, her savior, her friend. If fate had brought them together earlier, he might have saved her years of therapy! But she shuts up as her mother, now the avenging angel, fights on her husband's behalf.

"You never understood him, Alice. Never! He adored you. Why until that moment, he walked you ev-er-y sing-le ni-gh-t," each syllable meant to impress upon Alice her father's all-night labors.

"I thought I had a nurse," Alice tosses back.

"Why do you insist on taking me so literally? You know what I mean. On the nurse's nights out, it was he who walked you. I can assure you, Alice, I didn't. And it wasn't easy for him Alice. You did, after all, have colic!" a condition that now sounded like a venereal disease Alice had brought on herself. "He was so hurt, Alice. So hurt."

"Some sensitive man, your husband," Mr. Steiner chimes in.

Alice refrains from a loud, "Bravo!" "Mom, forget for the moment why I cried. Just think about the fact Dad was so hurt by some stupid remark, he kept his hands off me until I was almost two years old. Did you ever consider that maybe, by the time he decided to put them back on, I might not even have known who the hell he was?"

"There's no reason to swear, Alice. And that's ridiculous. How could you not know your own father? He'd been in the same house with you from the time you were born. "Oh, Alice," the sigh again. "All he wanted was your love, and you went and rejected him all over again."

Alice waits for support, but Mr. Steiner is silent. She goes it alone.

"Mom, listen to me! I could not have hated Dad when I was six months old. Even if he'd been abusing me physically, I couldn't have."

"Where in God's name did you get such an idea? Is that what that therapist of yours is filling your head with? That your father was a. . . a child abuser?"

"You don't look abused to me," Mr. Steiner pipes in.

"I'm not saying I was," Alice's voice rising as her affair with Mr. Steiner wanes. "But even an abused infant doesn't hate."

"My God! Alice, you were not abused. We gave you everything. Simply everything!" Her words shot over the divider so they reached Mr. Steiner right between the ears.

"I didn't say I was abused. Only that even an abused infant doesn't know from hatred. Fear, yes. Anxiety, yes. Even rage. But hatred, no!"

"I give up, Alice. I simply give up" and her mother retreats again to her window.

They pull up to the hospital. Her mother pays Steiner–any desire on Alice's part to slip him an extra tip dispelled by his lack of loyalty. She watches her mother propel herself to the elevators and follows steeling herself for what, or more accurately who, lies ahead. Her mother is already steeled. She marches down the hall, acknowledging those at the Nurse's Station with a nod of her head, stops, takes a mirror from her bag, freshens her lipstick, checks her hair, then pushes open the door, and goes over to the bed. Alice trails, stopping just inside the doorway.

"Look what they've done to me!" her father cries out. "Look!" He starts to weep. They look to where he's pointing–his arm, a mangled mess of bruised skin and sinew. The rest of what's left of him thankfully hidden under the sheet. "That *pishika* intern, he wouldn't listen. I told him not to touch me. But did he listen? Did he? No!"

"That's awful, Dad," Alice says even though she knows he won't acknowledge her presence. He hasn't for weeks though how long it's been this time, she has no idea. She stopped counting his silences long ago. His record being six months–if one doesn't consider the span of time between when she was six months and when she turned two.

"Take me home," he pleads to his wife. "Home!" He does not add "to die," but that's clearly what he means. They get the doctor's approval and a few hours later he's in his own bed.

Alice visits daily. It no longer matters that for years she worked at distancing herself from him emotionally, as well as physically. His impending death draws her like a magnet–remaining close less painful than staying away.

It's now day three. Her father is in a chair in the living room, her mother knitting, and Alice is straightening up the already straightened up, when she's not opening and closing the frig, as if there was something inside that could fill her emptiness. She has another hour of this until her brother Rich and his wife will spell her.

"I'm too tired for company," her father announces to no one in particular.

She decides to risk it. "I can call them. Tell them not to come."

"Did I tell you to do that?" His voice still more than capable of resonating threat.

"No," she says and retreats. At least he'd spoken directly to her, though she can't be certain if it's the end of a siege or one of his time outs. Over the years he's had many of these, momentarily breaking his silence if he needed her to do something.

"Then sit!"

Her mother's knitting needles click furiously as if each knit one, pearl one can keep the inevitable explosion at bay.

Suddenly her father's eyes soften. "Tell you what," he says. "Why don't you call your brother? Tell him I'm tired. Just pretend I don't know that you're calling so he won't be hurt." A pause, then, "Okay?"

"Okay," Alice says and goes to the phone. Her mother puts her knitting down and leaves the room. A few minutes later her father asks Alice to call for the nurse. The two of them help him into bed.

"Mom, Dad wants to say goodnight," Alice calls and her mother goes in for what will be the last time. She won't be able to watch him waste away.

Mother and daughter pick at dinner. Alice opens up the sofa bed for her mother in the den and grabs a pillow and blanket for herself to use on the living room couch. It makes no sense to go home. Every hour or so, she goes into check on him. He's breathing harder. The night nurse just shakes her head.

Upon waking, Alice goes to his room. His eyes open, he waves her towards him. As she gets close, his boney fingers grab her arm, and pull her ear to his mouth.

"Do you love me?" he rasps.

"Of course, Dad. I always have."

"That's all I ever wanted to hear," he says and closes his eyes. For the next five hours she holds his hand and strokes his head as the sounds of his death rattle fill the room. The nurse tells Alice the hearing is the last sense to go, so Alice talks. About everything and nothing. At some point she tells him it's okay to let go–she has no idea where she heard that line. Then, the nurse says something which causes Alice to turn away from him for a moment, and the room goes silent. Just like that! Hours of thrashing, years of thunder, over. In a split second.

Peace.

Coda

Days before her father's death, Alice sits next to the pulled-out sofa bed on which her mother lies exhausted. "You'll need to go soon," her mother says.

And Alice says she will, "As soon as Rich arrives." It makes her nervous to leave the house knowing her father could go at any time. It's just that she and her mom need black outfits and it's up to Alice to hunt some down. Weird. Two women in New York City and not a black dress between them. It had, after all, been eleven years since Helen died—she having forbidden them, as she battled cancer, to wear black, and the morning of the funeral Alice was forced to buy whatever she could find. If her father had called those dresses *shmatas*, he would have been dead on, but he was too beset by grief to care. Even so, Alice and her mom wore them throughout the eight-day shiva, shredded them the minute it was over, and had stayed away from buying black ever since. This time they were going to be prepared. Well, sort of.

The phone rings and Alice answers. It's her oldest friend, Dot, saying Jerry was in town. "He wants to talk, but doesn't think it's okay to call you at your mom's, considering."

"He's right. Have him call me at home, later. If there's no change here, I should be there after nine."

"Who?" her mom asked after Alice hung up.

"Jerry."

"He can call you here."

Her mom knows that Dot—wanting her two close friends to meet—had introduced them, that Jerry was on his third wife and that the three of them–Dot, Jerry and Alice—used to go to dinner, and

36

sometimes theater when he was in from the Coast. What she doesn't know about are the dinners without Dot, the weekends Jerry and Alice went away alone, the nights he stayed over. But then, omission has never been considered a lie in the Wallach household. "What someone doesn't know can't hurt them," a favorite expression of Alice's mother. Translation: please keep to yourself anything that might be upsetting, which is exactly what Alice had always done, at least up to the last few months. Then, whether because unconsciously she knew the mother-daughter relationship needed to change once her father was gone, or whether she was just tired of hiding her life, Alice found herself telling her mother small stuff. Like when she had a minor disagreement with a colleague. Or the difficulties she was experiencing with a particular patient—something she would never have considered doing before, concerned that her mother might think Alice lacking as a therapist. Even so, what comes out of her mouth in response to her mother's, "He can call you here," surprises even Alice.

"He's an old lover, Mom. It's been ages since we talked, and I don't want our first conversation to be here, especially now." There it was. Just like that. Hey, Mom, guess what? I'm not a virgin. And, surprise! Her mom doesn't die on the spot, she doesn't faint. She doesn't even gasp. Her immediate response, albeit in a voice filled with disappointment, "Oh, Alice, and here I swore to your father that you were a good girl."

Alice swallows the laugh that wants to erupt. "Mom, if by now I hadn't been to bed with a man, don't you think that would be something to worry about?"

Silence.

"Mom?"

"You know we never argued except where it concerned you."

"So you've told me—many times."

"Never."

"I know."

"And I defended you."

"I'm sure you did, Mom."

" Now, it seems he was right all along."

"That I wasn't a virgin or that I was a whore, or maybe a towel?" Her father's expression for any "loose" woman—as in something that men wipe their hands on.

"Alice, please. He never called you any of that."

"I bet." Alice had no trouble imagining her parents in deep discussion about her virginity. Her father's intrusiveness having been covered *ad nauseum* in her own therapy. But her mother defending her? Now that was something new.

Alice waits for what may come next. She doesn't have to wait long.

"If Jerry weren't married, would you have married him?"

She answers truthfully. "Not on your life. I prefer to be the cheated with, rather than the cheated on."

The doorbell rings. Alice, assuming it's Rich, grabs her purse, gives her mom a kiss on the forehead, and says she'll be back as soon as she finds them something to wear. Her mother doesn't move.

Alice greets her brother with, "Good luck!" and a hug, adding, "You're going to need it. She just found out I'm not a virgin."

"You're kidding!" Rich said.

"Not! She's all yours. I'm off to get us funereal garb."

Any resentments Alice held toward Rich have been dispelled by their father's impending death. For the past week, she's needed him to behave like the older brother (and dutiful son) he's supposed to be and he's complied. Coming up to see their dad daily, walking with Alice to pick up the morphine, even allowing his feelings to show.

"And Dad?" he calls as she heads out the door.

"Same." And with that, she leaves.

Two days later, on Wednesday, at 11:20p.m., Bertram Wallach dies. Not being observant Jews, the Wallachs, schedule his funeral for forty-eight hours later, allowing family, friends, business acquaintances of Rich's and colleagues of Alice's enough time to reschedule their lives so they can attend. As for Shiva, it lasts all of three afternoons, her mother deciding that would be as much as she was up to. "Your father wouldn't want me to get sick."

On the fourth day after the funeral, Alice arrives at her mom's to find her out on the three-by-four foot balcony that protrudes from the living room.

"I don't know why, but I love being out here," she calls to Alice.

"You couldn't get me out there for anything," Alice calls back. It has to do with her dislike of heights—her mother's apartment being on the fourteenth floor. (Actually, the thirteenth, but as with so many buildings in the city, its owners numbered the floors to make it appear as if the unlucky thirteenth didn't exist.)

"Well, I love it out here. Makes me feel free."

"I'm impressed."

"You know what would be nice?" her mom says as she comes in from the balcony. "Some of that green carpeting they advertise on TV. You know, the kind that looks like grass."

"You mean Astroturf?"

"Yes. I'd only need a small piece."

"John and Deb might have some, Mom. I can ask." Deb and Alice became friends years after John and Alice stopped seeing each other. The affair hadn't been long-term, but it was what pushed Alice into therapy–and eventually her profession. "I'll call her now," she adds and dials.

"Deb, it's me. Any extra Astroturf?" . . . "Oh, too bad." . . ." No, no problem. Mom wanted a small piece for her balcony." . . . "She's okay, thanks." . . . "I'll tell her. Talk soon. . ." "They threw the remnants away."

Then, as if all that had transpired—the death, the funeral, shiva—was nothing more than a stitch dropped from her knitting, her mom says, "And John, too?"

And Alice knows exactly to what her mom's referring. There's not a doubt in her mind. "I'm not going there, Mom," she says.

But her mom keeps knitting away, bringing up the name of every man Alice had ever mentioned, all with "bedded" in the form of a question mark attached: "Harvey Berenson?" "Everett Simon?" "Jack, oh what's his name?"

To all, Alice just smiles, and repeats, "Not saying, Mom. Besides, do you really want to know?" For the time being, there's just so much sharing Alice is prepared to do.

Last Wishes and All That

Ruth Wallach sits erect, her back pressed against the cab's cracked leather. "I'm sorry if I upset you, Alice."

"It's okay, Mom."

"It's just. . ."

"I said, it's okay."

The cab jerks forward, Alice presses her hand against the back of the front seat as her mother clings to the strap next to the window.

"I know cremation would make it easier for you," Ruth Wallach says. "But I really want to be near them." One has to choose one's words so carefully with Alice. She analyzes everything.

Alice Wallach finds the conversation stunning. A discussion about cremation versus internment? Now? Not more than twenty minutes after the doctor gave her mother three years to live?

"I said I don't mind, Mom," Alice's voice as tense as the muscles in her body. She tries to come to terms with what she's feeling, but ends up shoving her thoughts aside. They're not nice. Not nice at all.

"It's just I know how much you dislike cemeteries," Ruth Wallach continues. She's sorry to burden Alice with this, but she knows her daughter all too well. No matter what Alice says, she will mind. Her daughter is just too G.D. sensitive for her own good. Mrs. Wallach has never been able to curse. Even to herself.

"I have no problem with cemeteries, Mom."

Mrs. Wallach throws her daughter a look.

"Well, I don't," which was true. Alice enjoyed wandering through old cemeteries, imaging the lives lived from the dedications on the headstones. It was from the graves of those she knew that she kept her distance.

"It's just knowing I'll be with them gives me solace."

"I said its fine, Mom," her mother's sudden need for permission unnerving.

"Well, I'll tell Richard as well. Just so there are no discussions between you two later."

"There'll be no discussions," Alice's teeth are pressed so tightly together "discussions" comes out sounding like one long hiss. She knows no matter what her dear brother promises, when the time comes, he'll do whatever is expedient. How often did he show up when their dad was dying? Dashing in and out as if his failing heart was contagious–their mother buying his excuses about having to work. Some work! Most of the time, he was off screwing his secretary.

"Well, I'll tell him anyway, just to be sure."

Alice looks over at her mother. Amazing! The only sign her mother heard what the doctor said, was her fingers nervously playing with the clasp of her handbag. If a doctor had told Alice she had three years left, her nose would be red, there would be mascara dripping down her face, and she'd be jumping out of her skin, and down anyone and everyone's throat.

"You won't need to visit me there. I won't expect you," Mrs. Wallach adds.

Alice bites her lip, resisting the impulse to remind her Mom that once in the grave, she wouldn't know whether Alice visited or not. Instead, she comes out with something equally thoughtless. "Well, you never know, Mom. I could just surprise you." I could surprise you? Why couldn't she say something like, "Mom, you could change your mind," or "Mom, please! Have the operation then you could live forever." But no, all she can come up with is, "I could surprise you?" Dear God, what kind of a daughter is she? She knows the answer.

"Well, just as long as I'm next to your father."

Mrs. Wallach has been doing that a lot lately. Not getting off a subject. Even repeating herself. Often she doesn't know she has. Repeated herself. At least not until someone tells her. She resents people who do that. Remind her she's on her way to becoming old.

Especially when everyone takes her for years younger than she is. Although how old that is, she's not exactly sure. Mrs. Wallach doesn't know the year of her birth. Or her birthday for that matter. "I told you my birthday might be in January, didn't I?" she says.

"What?"

"My birthday. It might not be on Christmas Day."

"Yes, I know." All too well, Alice thinks, recalling all the years she, Rich and Helen were required to be present for all holidays, but especially their parents' anniversaries and birthdays—which because her grandmother shifted dates, included Christmas. A day Jews were not supposed to celebrate. A day it would have been fun to visit a friend who had a Christmas tree or perhaps take a long weekend away. Got to give it to Richard. "Do you think they really were married on Thanksgiving?" his reaction to their mother's revelation made ten years earlier outside an Emergency Room, as they waited to find out if Alice's father was going to live or die.

"Well, if my birthday is in January, then I'm a year younger," Mrs. Wallach now says.

Alice can't figure out what difference it makes.

"If my mother moved my birthday back a month, then I'm really a year younger," Mrs. Wallach says.

"So?"

"My brother said she did it so I could start school earlier."

"And?"

"I just wonder if I should tell the doctor. Tell him I'm not as old as I thought."

Dear God! Alice thinks, but says, "I don't think you need to, Mom," and wonders if they both are Capricorns after all.

Mrs. Wallach never understood why her own mother had kept it a secret. She certainly would have understood wanting one's children in school as early as possible. All right, maybe Mrs. Wallach didn't have as many children as her mother–three to her mother's six. But then her mother didn't have twelve years between the second and the last. She wishes Alice understood just how much they have in common, both being the babies of the family, but Alice has to be so

G.D. independent. Mrs. Wallach looks over at her daughter and lets out one long audible sigh.

Alice jumps. "What's wrong?"

"Nothing!" The last thing she needs is for Alice to start coddling her. She is not demented. She has a malfunctioning valve in her heart.

The cab inches forward. Alice realizes her foot has been pressed into the floorboard. She tries releasing it, but it won't relax. "Mom," she says. "You could have the operation." She has willed the words out, but they emerge as if by rote.

Mrs. Wallach shakes her head "no!"

"Well, you could. He said it's more than doable."

"I'm not having the operation, Alice."

Alice waits for her mother's usual "don't be childish" tag line, words Alice has heard from the time when it would have been appropriate for her to act like a child. Nothing comes and Alice's foot begins to ease up ever so slightly. "Well, just know you can change your mind," she says.

The other thing Mrs. Wallach knows about her daughter is that she'll miss her mother terribly. But that's also something Mrs. Wallach can't do anything about. "No operation. And no hospitals!" she orders. "For what? To play Bridge? With women I don't care about? I'm tired of them. The same conversations, The constant complaints. Enough!"

"But you said you loved Bridge. Always wanted to play it."

"I do. I just don't need to play it forever."

Both women's thoughts land simultaneously onto Mr. Wallach and his refusal to let Mrs. Wallach join a Bridge club. Bridge was an educated man's game. One he didn't believe he could learn.

They are now stuck in traffic. For a change, neither woman glances at the meter. Alice stares out of her window swatting away each thought as it rises to the surface. She should want her mother to live forever. Swat. If her mother opts for surgery, Alice would have to care for her. Swat, swat. Her mother's death could mean Alice would have the money to. . . swat Swat SWAT!

Mrs. Wallach's focus is on her gravestone.

Ruth Wallach, Beloved Wife, Mother.

Ruth Wallach, Beloved Wife, Mother and Mother-in-Law. Better. Lewis has been good to her, better in some ways than her own children.

Ruth Wallach, Beloved Wife of Bertram Wallach, Mother to Helen Wallach Strauss, Richard Wallach and Alice Wallach. Mother-in Law to Lewis and Phyllis Strauss, and Lauren Wallach. No! A complete waste of money. She hasn't watched what she's spent these last years, only to have it pissed away. She can't believe that word had crossed her mind. She always hated it when Bertram used it. Well, she had to admit, there wasn't really a better way to put it. She wasn't going to piss away her money. Piss piss piss. Mrs. Wallach decides on Ruth Wallach, Beloved Wife, Mother, and Mother-in-Law. Born 1902–probably her real birth date. Died? Three years from now. 1986. Done! She will put it in writing and give it to Lewis. He'll see to it. See that it's done.

Mrs. Wallach wonders if she'll see her parents after she dies. She pictures her mother seated in their living room, mirror in hand, applying lipstick, over and over again, no matter who was in the room. Mrs. Wallach does not want to end up like her. Wants to go before her mind does. She feels guilty she hasn't visited her own parents' graves for years. Except that one time with Alice right after Bertram died. They'd traipsed, for what seemed like ages, through the dilapidated cemetery until she found them. Bert had been right, of course. Every year he said she should stop wasting money paying for perpetual care. But they were her parents, so she paid. Besides, she paid all their bills. Handled their money from the day she and Bert married and he admitted he couldn't read or write English. How he hid in their bedroom when her friends visited, embarrassed by his accent. But she'd taught him. Helped him as he went from company to company, selling his wares, sitting in the car, writing down the orders. And the marriage had worked. For fifty-four years. And she was envied. He was so handsome. Next week, she thinks.

"Next week what?" Alice asks.

"What?"

"Next week what?" Alice asks again.

Mrs. Wallach wonders how Alice could read her mind? Had she spoken aloud? "I was thinking I could visit your father."

"Sure, if you want."

"Richard or Lewis can take me. You could come."

"I'll pass." Not having a car has saved Alice from this particular trek over the years. She never could understand what her mother got from going. She didn't appear to find solace when they went to visit her parents' graves, grandparents who died before Alice was born. Guilt for not going sooner was all Alice saw. She and her mom had plowed through the overgrown bushes and overturned headstones until they found two mounds with two small slabs. Then her mom picked up some pebbles and placed them on the graves. "It's to show we've been here," her mom said. And Alice followed suit. "I would have come sooner, but your father never liked when I visited my family," and Alice had no doubt she meant whether they were alive or dead. It was then that it dawned on Alice how much more than her maiden name her mother had given up.

"Lewis bought four graves you know." Mrs. Wallach says.

"What?"

"Lewis. He bought four graves."

"I know, Mom."

"Two for Helen and him and two for us."

"Right."

"Not many son-in-laws would do that."

"No they wouldn't."

"He also pays the upkeep."

"Mom, can we talk about something else? Dr. Mastrelli didn't say you were going to die tomorrow." What the hell is wrong with me, Alice wonders. If her mother needs to talk, then she should let her talk. Alice knows that, she's been trained to listen.

"Never mind, I'll discuss it with Richard."

Damnit! thinks Alice.. It's the God damn piano all over again. . .

Eighteen years earlier, and a year and seven months after Helen, the Wallach's first born had died, Mrs. Wallach asked Alice to meet her for lunch. Having lunch together was not a rare event; having it by invitation was. The lunch was to take place at a coffee shop on Madison Avenue near the Wallach's home. Alice no longer lived there. She had moved out some six years earlier.

"My God! He actually let you out of his sight!" was how Alice greeted her mother. "What did you do, promise him we wouldn't smile?"

"Alice, please," said Mrs. Wallach as the manager led them to a booth. Her hushed voice meant to silence her daughter from saying anything more. One never knows who is listening or who knows who.

Mrs. Wallach would never admit it except to the one person who was no longer with them, but the lunch gave her a welcome respite from Mr. Wallach's mourning their daughter, and Mrs. Wallach's best friend– the relationship, between the two women cemented, the moment Mrs. Wallach realized there would be no competing with the child for Mr. Wallach's attention, and she made the conscious decision to become one with her daughter. Far better both bask in his adoration, than for her, Mrs. Wallach, to be relegated to a position of second best. Besides, it was a wife's job to keep her husband happy. Something Mrs. Wallach had never been able to drum into Alice's head. Well, at least she, Mrs. Wallach, had done her job well. She prided herself on how well she handled her husband. She'd even been able to do so, albeit with far more maneuvering, after Helen became ill, and Mr. Wallach retired, so he could be available to Helen's beck and call. Beckoning calls their daughter made only because she knew how much he needed her to need him. Once Helen was gone, he was left with nothing to do but mourn which, even Mrs. Wallach had to admit, he did with a vengeance.

The manager put down the menus on the table and the two women slid in.

Mrs. Wallach was already overcome by exhaustion and lunch hadn't even started. It was always like this. She couldn't remember a time when there was peace. "If you would only learn how to handle him, Alice, your life would be much easier."

"Sorry, he's all yours."

"Just stop putting me in the middle."

"Mom, Helen was your daughter too, and you haven't ordered life cease around you."

"I will not have you say another word against your father, Alice. Do you hear?"

"Fine! I'll have a hamburger and French fries. And a coke"

The waitress came over and Mrs. Wallach ordered for them both. Alice began to fold into accordion pleats the paper from the straw the waitress had tossed on the table.

"Please stop that, you're making me nervous."

Suddenly both women preferred to be elsewhere. Any fantasy of a fun mother-daughter lunch dashed. Mrs. Wallach searched for a subject which wouldn't cause additional upset. But what was there? Alice's refusal to compromise where men were concerned? Her going back to school to become a therapist? Everything Mrs. Wallach thought of would only lead to more consternation. She decided to get it over with. To get to the point–the reason she'd called the lunch in the first place.

"Alice. I need to talk to you about something and I don't want you getting upset."

Alice's stomach gripped. She wondered what the hell she had done wrong now.

"What?" she said, inhaling through the straw.

"Your father and I need to make out a new will now that your sister's gone and well, we want to know what you want."

The coke went right through Alice's nostrils. "I don't want anything, Mom," she snorted.

"This is serious. The silver? The good dishes? You are the only girl now and someday you might get married and should decide what you would want."

"And you'll still be here if and when I do. For God's sake, Mom! You're not going to die. At least not for a long time. Besides, there's nothing I want."

Mrs. Wallach took a bite out of her burger and repeated her request. "This is not about us dying, this is about making out our will and we need to know what you want."

"I said I don't want anything. And once again, you are not going to die."

It went on this way throughout the meal. More accurately, throughout Mrs. Wallach's meal. Alice's burger sat on her plate, the coke, interspersed with a fry, all she could tolerate. By the time Mrs. Wallach ordered coffee and a piece of apple pie for them to share, Alice decided she was tired of being reassuring. There was something she wanted. She didn't have room for it where she lived now, but could someday. And it was hers, really. No one else ever played it. Granted she never was that good, but still. . . "All right," she said. "I want the piano."

Mrs. Wallach wiped her mouth with her napkin and shook her head. "Well, we will have to discuss it with Rich, he is the oldest and if he wants it. . .

"You don't need to discuss it with Rich, mom. It's your piano, do with it as you want."

Mrs. Wallach turns to look out her window again as the cab moves forward. In three years she'll be lying next to her husband. Not that she will actually be next to him. But close enough. Like in twin beds. She smiles. It's what they'd always had. Twin beds. Young people nowadays don't know how much fun they can be. Climbing from one to another as if by special invitation. "Whose side do you think I'll be on?" she asks.

"What?" Alice says.

"Which side? Your father's or Helen's?"

"You've got to be kidding." Alice says.

"I just want to know if the two empty graves are on Helen's side or your father's."

"Why, for God's sake?"

"Because! I want to be next to him. And I know he would like to be between the two of us."

"I'm sure he would," Alice mutters. Then, "I'm sure that's how it will work out, Mom. Helen went in first, then Dad, and when the time comes, you'll be next to Dad."

"But then Lewis will be next to me. I'm sure he would want to be next to Helen."

"Mom, maybe Lewis will want to be near Phyllis, which means he won't want the grave."

"Oh! Well, if you don't marry, you could take it." A thought she wished she'd kept to herself–the idea of spending eternity making peace between Alice and her father too exhausting to imagine.

"I could, but I won't." No way she would spend eternity with her family. Cremation for her. Ashes tossed off the Empire State Building, or any roof top for that matter.

The cab nears her mother's building. Alice glances at her watch. 1:30. No wonder she's starved. The cab stops. Her mother pays. The doorman opens the cab's door.

"What would you like for lunch?" Mrs. Wallach asks, nodding to the doorman as she heads towards the building.

"What is there?"

"Eggs. A can of tuna. If you want something else, you'll need to go to the store."

"I'll go to the store after I get you upstairs."

"I'm not dying Alice. Go! Get us both turkey sandwiches. On rye. Unless you want something else.

"No that's fine."

"And maybe some coleslaw."

"Anything else?"

"Not unless you want something." Mrs. Wallach reaches into her bag for a ten.

Alice takes the money and watches her mother walk inside. Three years more, she thinks. Three years more.

The Fifth Question

Alice leaves her apartment, her usual quick long strides now recalcitrant slogs weighted down by resentment–the roots easily identifiable. She's to be deprived of her Seder. The one night a year she looked forward to, the way children look forward to Christmas. Not that she'd ever been to a real Passover Seder. One of those by the book, three-hour prayer-filled, wine sipping, when-will-the-food-ever-appear, affairs. And not that she's religious. More like an agnostic Jew. One who rails against the exclusionary aspects of all religions, mezzuzahs on doorposts, religious symbols hung from necks in obscene fashion statements. Even so, it never stopped her from secretly hoping that this Passover would be the one when specters of Seders past could appear.

Each year, as she watched ladles of matzah ball soup, pieces of gefilte fish, slices of pot roast, the endless servings of potato kugel, and slabs of flourless strawberry shortcake, devoured, she would yearn for the times her father rose from his seat at the head of the table, the white yarmulka on his head, his white and blue prayer shawl draped over his shoulder, and begin to doven, as if moved by an inner spirit. He would rock back and forth, intoning, in ritualistic fashion, the words of the Haggadah, while simultaneously demanding the attention of everyone in the room. *Where had he learned those notes, those incantations? She should have asked. Too late now–the answers were buried with him.* Oh, the illicit glee as Lewis and Rich cracked jokes beneath their breath, Helen pretended to admonish them, and their mother desperately tried to contain her laughter, only to have her face turn red, tears stream from her eyes, and giggles break through her lips like irrepressible bubbles. For it was on that night, that one night only, Alice's father's fiery sparks of disapproval, miraculously bounced off all around him without doing harm. It was also the night when Alice, as the youngest, would be asked to stand and recite the four questions, that is, until her sister's children came of age, and took over the role. Then came Helen's illness, her death, and everything changed.

Alice opted for a bus over the subway, having assumed the bus would fly up the avenue. In the past, the city seemed to empty out as Jews raced home to ready themselves for the feast. After a few blocks she realized the traffic was no different on this night from any other rush hour, the bus having quickly filled up with people going about their business, as if the day were nothing special. Where had the Jews gone? Swallowed up by assimilation? By the suburbs? Possibly. Wasn't Westchester where she had Seder ever since her dad died? Where she should have been tonight? Childish. Even if she had gone to Westchester, her fantasy would have been dispelled soon enough. Reality always set in once Lewis, without his first father-in-law's censorial presence, breezed through the service. Poor Phyllis. Hours spent preparing the Seder plate, the special foods, the table, all to have it over within a flash.

It wasn't as if Alice's mother hadn't given her the option. "It's all right, dear. I have the aide. Go to Phyllis's if you want." But there was no way Alice could. Not with Rich off in Florida pretending to be a dutiful husband. "No, Mom," she'd answered. "We'll have our own Passover. What do you want me to bring?" And her mother had said the aide would pick up dinner. That she already had matzahs and gefilte fish in the house. Not to worry. "Just come." If Helen were alive, she would have parted the Red Sea to bring the Seder, yamulkas and all, to their mother. Cater the whole thing herself. That's what Helen would do, did. Cater. Round the clock. One call of mild distress from their mother, and Helen would leave hearth, home, husband and children, to play caretaker. Maybe that's why she got sick. Saw no other way to leave the family business. Could never stop catering. What had her mother said? "I always knew your father loved your sister more than anything in this world. That's why I became her best friend." She'd said that to Alice, shortly after his death, thankfully over the phone, saving Alice from having to hide her incredulousness. Not that Alice hadn't known that Helen and their mother were tied at the hip. It was just that Alice had assumed their bond started in the womb, was reinforced at first sight, then grew until it wove them both into an inseparable unit, leaving very little room for Alice to maneuver.

Alice was now late, the bus having crawled up the avenue. When she finally arrived, she hurried past the doorman into the elevator, her tension rising with every floor. She steeled herself at the door, expecting her mother's usual welcoming exuberance—those beaming eyes and grateful smile that demanded more from Alice than she could emotionally return. How the tables had turned. Now it was her mother who sought love and affection. "A hug-a-day keeps the doctor away," she'd say on Alice's arrivals and departures. And Alice would smile and awkwardly comply, bringing her arms around her mother's now slight frame, in a stilted embrace. But then, Alice couldn't remember ever being held by her mother, their only moments of physical contact coming years ago, when on the way home from Helen's or Richard's, in the back seat of the car, Alice, exhausted, would rest her head on her mother's lap, and her mother's distracted fingers would play with Alice's hair.

She rang the bell, waited, then rang again. Eventually the door opened, only instead of her mother, there stood an aide Alice had not seen before, weirdly bowing and scraping in exaggerated circus-like fashion. "Come in, come in, see what we have for you!" she said, scaring the hell out of Alice. Alice followed the woman through the living room towards the dining alcove only to find her mother, clad in the pink terrycloth robe normally worn only after her morning bath, slouching, her back towards the room as the aide called out, "Your daughter's here. Your daughter's here." Her Jamaican lilt turning her words into a Calypso song. Only Alice's mother didn't turn around. Nor did she raise her eyes towards the mirrored wall to see who was behind her.

Dear God! Where was the woman they had playfully labeled "The Queen"? The woman who had never gone down the hall to a neighbor's not fully groomed? The woman who at eighty-six still paid attention to the latest fashion? Why was she displaying herself in such disarray, paying no mind to her untied robe, the nightgown falling off her shoulders, breast exposed and her hair looking as if the brush had missed its mark?

"Mom!" Alice cried, lunging towards her mother as she began to slip off the chair, and only barely managing to catch her just before she fell to the floor. "Mom, are you alright?"

No answer.

"Mom," Alice repeated, as much to get her mother's attention as to assure herself this woman was actually her mother. "Mom, it's me."

And then, from nowhere, "Of course it's you, dear, who would it be? Did you say hello to Orin? Orin, this is my daughter. We're going to have Seder." Said as if Alice's world hadn't just been turned into a scrambled jigsaw puzzle that would never fit together again.

Alice looked down at the table with its missing damask tablecloth, forks placed where the knives should be, and three mismatched plates instead of her mother's good china. Yes, there were matzahs and Gefilte fish, but the matzahs were still in the box, the fish in a jar. And while there was a Pyrex dish filled with something that resembled haroset, there was no Seder plate, no Haggadahs, not even her mom's silver candelabra with candles for her to light–her mother having always lit candles on holidays, and even on some Friday nights. She'd stand, a white damask napkin on her head, and wave her hands over the flames. Then she'd put her fingers over her eyes and recite the Sabbath prayer in Hebrew, and when her hands came down, her eyelids were red, and Alice would have to fight back her own sobs that always followed her mother's tears.

Alice looked down at her mother's hands moving erratically along the table's edge like long spidery legs frantically trying to escape. The fingers were still long, the nails beautiful, the polish Alice had applied a few days ago still on.

"Mom, do you want something to eat?"

"That would be nice, dear."

Alice went into the kitchen. There was a rotisserie chicken, but nothing else. It wasn't that Alice expected her mother to cook. The family joke was that her mother couldn't even boil water until after Alice's father died. Then she would call Alice each night so Alice could talk her through how to broil a lamb chop, or a piece of fish. "Try it Mom," she'd say. "If you louse it up, you can always make scrambled eggs." No, she hadn't expected her mother to cook, but she would have expected her to send the aide out for more than just a chicken. Alice put the chicken on a platter and brought it to the table as her mother whispered into the aide's ear and they both broke into giggles. Then, her mom turned to Alice. "Sit down, dear. Sit down and tell Orin about the seder, dear. About this. Tell her about this!"

"It's haroset, Mom," Alice said, not knowing whether to be scared or horrified and so was neither.

"And this, tell Orin what this is."

"It's a matzah."

"Well, tell her what a matzah is."

And Alice, who long ago had sat in nervous anticipation of the moment when her father would shush all around the table so that Alice could ask, "Mah nish-ta-nah hal-lai-lah haz-zeh mik-kol hal-le-lot. . . Why is this night different from all other nights? On all other nights we eat leavened bread. Why on this night do we eat matzah? Why do we dip the parsley in salt water and the bitter herbs in haroset? And why on this night do we recline at the table. . ." And she, who had so proudly recited the Four Questions, now wanted to scream the answers. "Because on this night, God, on this night, my mother is losing her mind, and I am losing my mother, and I will no longer be a child, her child, anyone's child. The bitter herbs are mine. The tears of the salt water mine, and now I'm in this madhouse about to tell my mother's new playmate about matzah, haroset and the Seder, words my mother can no longer find."

Alice thought of calling her brother to get his ass back up from Florida. But what would that do? The doctor said her mom had three years when she opted out of having her valve replaced three years ago. He never told them by not having the operation her mind would go before her breath.

Alice's mother was now moving her eyes between the chandelier overhead and Alice as if trying to force her to look upward. Then, suddenly, she curled her body snakelike towards her daughter and looking like a four year old with a delicious secret, asked, "Would you like to know how you were conceived? You were a love child, you know."

Alice couldn't move. Those words. Now?

"Well, you were."

"So you've always said, Mom." And her mother had. For as long as Alice could remember. Not that it ever made sense. Not to a child who had been brought up by nursemaids, cleaning ladies and cooks. Whose parents went on vacations for weeks that could turn into months. Who sent their daughter to sleep away camp at age three. Love child? How do you mesh together that phrase with all the tales of a woman who, upon finding herself pregnant, had sat in darkened movie theaters, so she could tell her husband it was the sad stories that had made her cry?

"A love child," her mother repeated. Then, in between giggles, those darting eyes and fingers that wouldn't stop moving, out it came with astonishing clarity. "I had just finished decorating our bedroom, when your father came home. He got so excited, so thrilled with what I had done, he wanted, well, you know. . ."

Alice held her breath not knowing what to expect as the spidery fingers now crawled onto her sweater and pulled her close.

"He wanted it right then and there," her mother whispered, the "it" barely audible. Her lips causing a tingling sensation in Alice's ear. "I begged him to stop. Pleaded with him it was the wrong time of the month, but he wouldn't listen. Just took me. Right then and there. "Right under this very chandelier."

Alice pulled away so she could see her mother's face. But instead of her mother showing signs of distress, she was smiling. Broadly. Certainly not the look of someone who had just described a rape.

"It used to hang in our bedroom, remember? Over our beds. I tried to get to the bathroom, to get some protection, but he wouldn't hear of it. So see! I always told you, you were a love child. And you never believed me!"

Alice slowly let out her breath and closed her eyes. There was her parents' bedroom. The vanity table with its satin skirt where her mother applied her makeup and Alice brushed her mother's hair, the twin beds covered with silver satin covers and above them, the same chandelier, with its crystals that cast their magical lights onto the pale celadon walls. And there, crosswise on the bed, lay her mother, Alice's father on top.

Alice opened her eyes, pulled herself up and began to rearrange the table so it looked a bit more presentable. She took out the good napkins and placemats from the drawer. She reset the table with the good silverware and nice dishes. She set the matzah on a dish and the fish on a platter. With the silver serving spoon she offered the aide a piece of fish and placed one on her own. Then she laid her hand gently on her mother's fingers, gave her mother a kiss on the cheek, picked up a fork, and began putting small bites of gefilte fish into her mother's mouth.

Appearances

It was rather incredible how matter-of-fact Mrs. Bloom had been. Not like the other women, her mother's lately acquired widowed friends, with their "She was a beautiful woman," "Such fun," "We'll miss her" spoken in tones of sincere condolence, as each wondered who among them would be next. Only Mrs. Bloom had put it out there as she sat down next to Alice on the small purple-cushioned bench, her white hair unencumbered by a hat or veil.

"The only thing wrong with your mother, dear, was that she took your father so seriously." Just like that! As if Alice had known it all along. "Now, I didn't mean it in a derogatory way," Mrs. Bloom quickly added, perhaps having interpreted Alice's look of momentary confusion as her having taken offense . "Your mother was a dear friend. I'm simply stating what was. Your father was, well, you know... And your mother, well... She always just went along." All this while off in the next room, Alice's mother lay nestled in white satin, in the brass-handled mahogany casket that was blanketed by white roses.

Mrs. Bloom's remark flitted around Alice's brain like a fly that refused to leave no matter how often it's swatted away. It wasn't as if she hadn't always known her mother's life revolved around her husband. She had put him way before herself or her children. But Alice sensed Mrs. Bloom's remark held other implications, although what they were exactly she couldn't quite put her finger on.

Alice sat on the floor of the apartment sorting through what remained of her parents' possessions. It was what, fourteen–no, fifteen years ago when she helped her mother unpack many of the same items she was now deciding whether to keep, toss or give away.

She and her brother, well, really her sister-in-law having already divvied up the main pieces—Rich preferring to sell the whole lot– "We didn't have it before, who the hell needs it now?" But there were things from Alice's childhood she wasn't ready to relinquish to memory, so, with Rich's wife coveting much of the silver, Mr. Doyle, the man hired to settle the estate, suggested they toss a coin and, like team captains picking players, have at it. Lauren won the toss and laid claim to the Tiffany platter, Alice, a Tiffany bowl, Lauren, the hall mirror, Alice a bronze lamp, Lauren the sterling serving pieces, Alice the sterling flatware–ignoring her sister-in-law's remark, about Alice having no need of it as she never entertained, "certainly not formally."

The only real battle came over the ornate silver grape scissors that no longer cut. "You can't have those," Alice said. "But it's my turn and that's what I want," countered her sister-in-law, and Alice, who had been trying to keep it all together, uncharacteristically exploded. "They're mine, damnit! They're part of my childhood, not yours, not Rich's, mine!" But her sister-in-law took Alice's outburst personally and dug in her heels. Alice, regaining control, tried to make her sister-in-law understand that creating the centerpieces for her parents' dinner parties held great significance for her, and the scissors were a part of that. Arranging the fruit in the large green and white porcelain bowl–long disappeared– then draping the large bunches of grapes so they hung over the sides, interspersing leaves cut from flowers her mother had placed around the house, and then, the final touch: those scissors. "For heaven's sake, Lauren, I don't have that many great memories." Mr. Doyle stepped in and resolved the dispute by promising Lauren a new pair as a gift. The fact they turned out to be far more exquisite than the ones they were arguing over, did not bother Alice in the least. She had hers. That's what was important.

Alice looked around. The room now a replica of when her parents first moved in: rugs rolled up in the corner; paintings Alice had grown up with stacked against the wall, boxes packed with glassware, dishes and chotchkes, strewn about. The apartment so full of expectancy then, barren now. Alice dropped the last of the white-on-white damask tablecloths into a box with a blue sticker: blue for Goodwill, black for the auction house, red for her to keep. Items for the cleaning lady, her mother's night nurse, and a neighbor, tagged with their names—Lauren already having carted off her haul. Alice wondered if maybe there wasn't something of her mother's she might give to Mrs. Bloom. An initialed handkerchief, maybe. Not that Alice could imagine an 86-year-old wanting another memento her own daughter would eventually have to give away. Alice remembered how her mother, shortly after her diagnosis, stopped the paring down she'd begun a few years earlier. Almost like she could keep death at bay by making certain everything stayed in place.

As if feeling for a pulse, Alice took note of her numbness. She hated this part of the mourning process, the psyche's way of avoiding pain. She knew the more benumbed she felt now, the more pain to come. She'd experienced the same thing after her father died. Walking along the street, convinced life was back to normal and then, from nowhere, being engulfed by a huge wave of sadness or a bout of weeping. Other times sideswiped by moments of intense dislocation where everything around seemed to disappear. She wondered how Mrs. Bloom dealt with it all. It couldn't be easy for a woman her age to bury the last of her friends. Perhaps her taking a jab at Alice's mother was her way of coping. It might make an interesting subject for Alice to assign her class: "The Mourning Process as Experienced by Those in Various Stages of Life."

Alice rose and went to the hall closet, as much to clean it out, as to stop an onset of "the guilts." She had thought they would end, once her mother was gone. But no, just remembering her dreams of freedom from her mother's ever-mounting needs, brought them back full force. But no, they were still there. Guilt brought on by her dreams of freedom from her mother's ever-mounting needs. It wasn't that Alice hadn't physically done all she could, she just hadn't done it with unmitigated devotion.

Alice couldn't decide which to tackle first. The hatboxes filled with God-knows-what or the coats, what there were of them, on the gold-leafed hangers engraved with the letter "W." Rich thought her crazy when she asked if he wanted them. "We have enough crap," his response. "Fine, then I'll take them." Alice removed her mother's favorite coat from its hanger, a magenta mohair she'd convinced her mother to buy.

"Your father would never approve, Alice. I mean it's magenta!"

"So?"

"He'd think it's way too... I don't know, loud, too something."

"Well, he's not here, Mom, and you look fantastic in it."

And she had. She'd glowed. The same as when Alice was nine and her mother brought home a magnificent rose taffeta evening gown, with a huge silk flower tucked under the folds of its skirt gathered up at the side like a cancan dancer's. Alice had watched her mother float around the apartment, humming made-up melodies, filling the house with magic. The perfect fairy godmother. All she needed was a wand and glass slippers. Then Alice's father came home and drenched the moment with his mood. Not that Alice could recall what was said, but she clearly remembered how her mother wilted, and the dress came off never to be seen again. Like a bad artist, her father was an expert at overworking a canvas until its once-brilliant colors turned to mud.

The more her father tried to mold Alice into his image of the perfect woman, the more resistant to change she became. She would be accepted as is. No modifications. No enticements. Nails unpainted. Makeup unnecessary. Bras, when she wore one, that added nothing to her modest breasts. Her hair cut only when it became too unwieldy to gather into the knot she'd worn for as long as she could remember—her entire look a refutation of her mother's acquiescence to his version of perfection. Had Mrs. Bloom known about her father's intrusion into her mother's presentation of self? Probably not. Alice couldn't imagine her mother saying one negative word about her husband to anyone.

The men Alice chose seemed not to be concerned about looks. Her latest, Bill, a prime example. No physical demands on her appearance. To the contrary, he could be oblivious even when she wanted him to take notice. It wasn't as if they didn't have a reasonable sex life. Just that Alice sometimes wondered if arousal came from their respective hormonal needs, never mind any real physical attraction. Alice changed her mind and decided the hangers were going to Goodwill. She didn't need reminding that the "W" still worked for her. Not that she could ever imagine changing her name for anyone, but still.

What would Mrs. Bloom think, Alice wondered? To know her father's presence, so formidable while he was alive, had been reduced to one photograph in a nine-by-six silver frame, a pair of gold cufflinks, and a watch she'd never seen him wear, found in a drawer? For someone who had once filled the space with demands—whether spoken or implied–to be reduced to the top of a table off to the side of the living room... well, wouldn't Mrs. Bloom find that more than just a little interesting?

Alice had always admired Mrs. Bloom, even before the Blooms had become weekly fixtures in her parents' lives. How could she not? From the time Alice could remember, Mrs. Bloom had been extolled. "She's a college graduate," her mother would say, or, "She's always reading," or, "You know, she worked in an office even after she was married, when she obviously didn't need to!" By the time Alice was born, both couples had found their way into the closed society of upper-middle class West Side Jewish life. Whether the Blooms had done better financially, Alice couldn't be certain. If they had, it was probably because they didn't spend so much on redecorating, expensive suits, new clothes, new cars. Of course that's not how Alice's mother would have seen it. "You either have style or you don't," is what she would have said.

One by one, Alice began pulling down the hatboxes. "Oh God, Mother! You've got to be kidding," she said aloud, as if her mother were still in the room. Not that finding the boxes empty should have surprised. "There's enough to be depressed about in this world, without adding to it," her mother say. "If seeing the boxes, empty or not, makes me feel good, why not?" And why not indeed? Hadn't her mother filled the two narrow book cases in their den with books no one ever read?

Alice removed her mother's remaining evening gown from its plastic bag. Layers of black chiffon with large imprinted pink flowers on satin lining, bought for a cruise two years after Alice's father died—a dress Alice could neither have fit into nor found occasion to wear. It had to go. As should the beautiful suits her mother had crocheted, but these Alice decided to keep– the thought of running into someone wearing one too awful to imagine.

The phone rang. It would be Bill calling to find out when she was going to be finished. She, too, was surprised by how long it was taking. Her normal style to bulldoze her way through a project, "getting it over and done with" often outweighing how well it was carried out.

"Not done yet?" An edge to his voice.

"Getting there."

"You're torturing yourself."

"Once it's gone, it's gone, Bill."

"You didn't even like your mother's taste, so why hold onto the stuff now? Just toss it into boxes and get the hell out of there. You've been up there every night for two weeks."

She didn't know why she couldn't just pack it all up. All she knew was that she felt compelled to do this one last chore for her mother as her mother would have wanted it done.

"I'm keeping the silver."

"I thought you said you could get a lot for it."

"I know. But I've been eating with it since I was a child."

"Not since I've known you, you haven't."

"I did when I came up here."

"Right. And you're going to polish it."

"Maybe."

"Sure you will," his voice peeved.

"Bill?"

"What?"

"There are no robes left."

"What?"

"No robes."

"Jesus! You planned to wear her bathrobes?"

"No. I mean, I just wish there was one."   The last of her mother's terry cloth robes, indelibly stained, tossed into the garbage the week before her death. Robes worn, starting when Alice was a little girl, after her mother's morning bath, as she phoned the butcher, grocer, vegetable man to order the evening's meal. But it was the cocktail ones, Alice missed.

"I'm coming up there and we'll get this finished," Bill said.

"No!" She hadn't meant to sound so adamant. "I'm sorry," she said, feeling the first sob bubbling up. Not yet. Not yet.   "I'll be home soon, promise."

Alice didn't expect to find her favorites. "Mom, there are only two in the closet," she'd said shortly after her father died.

"Two's enough."

"But you had so many."

"Well, I don't need more now that your father's not here to enjoy them."

"But you loved those robes."

"Your father loved me in those robes, Alice."

"But didn't you love them? What about that green satin one? With the coral sash? And the beautiful lining. The coral lining." The one that had transformed her mother into a courtesan in Alice's eyes.

"It was pretty, wasn't it?"

"How could you give it away?"

"Why keep it? For whom?"

"For you!"

"Oh, Alice. I said your father loved the robes and I loved him. When will you understand?". . .

Alice tried to imagine herself dashing home from wherever, running a bath, reapplying her makeup and slipping into a cocktail robe to greet Bill at the door, hors d'oeuvres and drinks waiting, the way her mother had done for her father almost every day of their married life. Bill would think she'd lost her mind, if he even noticed.

Alice picked up her mother's address book and started leafing through the pages. She could almost trace her mother's decline. The older entries in her mother's perfect cursive script, the newer ones, mostly names of doctors, tentative, slightly erratic. She turned back to the Bs and dialed. There was a lot she needed to ask Mrs. Bloom.

"Why, how nice to hear from you, Alice," Mrs. Bloom answered, sounding pleased, though not so pleased as to make Alice feel she'd be sucked into picking up groceries, or running errands, or simply keeping her company. Just a "How nice to hear from you" and a concerned "How are you doing?" Along with "I was so sorry your mother and I were not able to get together more."

Alice knew her mother and Mrs. Bloom hadn't seen much of each other the last few years. It wasn't that the friendship had waned. Simply that their situations had changed.

"You know, it was hard with Mr. Bloom being ill and all. Then by the time he passed, your mother got sick. And, well, you know your mom. She would never let anyone see her not at her best. A shame really."

Alice wondered what Mrs. Bloom was referring to—her mother's concern about appearances or Mrs. Bloom's not getting to see her?

"Mom understood that you also had your hands full," she said. Which wasn't true: her mother had been terribly hurt that the Blooms hadn't invited her over more after Alice's father died.

"Mom, how often did you invite Mrs. Cohn or Mrs. Greenblatt after their husbands died?" she'd asked.

"Well, I couldn't. You know your father. He hated being surrounded by all those widows. Reminded him he might be next."

"Could it be the same with Mr. Bloom?"

Alice wished she could have taken that back. Sooth out the shock on her mother's face as she'd realized she was now officially "one of them."

"I was wondering if you would like to have lunch sometime, Mrs. Bloom."

"Why isn't that sweet of you, Alice," Mrs. Bloom replied. "That would be nice. But you mustn't feel you have to or anything. I know how busy you are."

"Mrs. Bloom, I wouldn't ask if I didn't want to. How about I call after I've finished with mom's apartment?"

"I'll look forward to hearing from you. But again, don't think you must. I have plenty to keep me busy."

And Alice had no doubt she did. Her reading. Her interests. "Mrs. Bloom?"

"Yes, dear?"

"What did you mean about Mom taking Dad so seriously?"

"Well, she did."

"So you said, but. . . Never mind. We'll talk over lunch."

"I'd love that, dear."

"Me, too."

Rich thought her crazy. "Why would you want to do that?" he asked.

"She knows things. Has history."

"You really are nuts!" His easy response to anything that made him uncomfortable. "Any normal person would take some time off from death and dying."

"Mrs. Bloom is anything but dying, Rich."

"She's as old as our mother was."

"And her heart is just fine. I bet she'd like to see you, Rich."

"Thanks, but no thanks," he'd said.

She wasn't surprised. Attachments weren't his thing.

When she told Bill, he just shrugged. It was her life.

Mrs. Bloom was waiting in the lobby of the pre-war apartment building on West End Avenue, where the Blooms had lived since Alice could remember. They never moved across the park to the East Side, the way her parents did. Alice could just imagine her mother's reaction to the suit Mrs. Bloom was wearing. Very B. Altman's she'd say. Not like her mother's—always understated but very Bergdorf's.

"It's sweet of you to meet me here, Alice. I'm not as steady on my feet anymore."

"My pleasure." And it was. A sort of guilty pleasure. She'd been looking forward to seeing Mrs. Bloom in a way she hadn't looked forward to seeing her mother.

Mrs. Bloom leaned gently on Alice's arm as they walked up to the diner.

"Are you sure you don't want to go somewhere a little bit more special?" Alice asked.

"Oh no. I've been going there for years. Mr. Bloom liked me to get out at least once a day, even when he couldn't. Besides, I told them I'd be in today and if we didn't go, they'd be worried."

Alice shook her head. She tried to imagine her mother leaving her father in the house alone–leaving him in a room alone for more than a few minutes could provoke a loud, "Dear! Where are you?"

Mrs. Bloom had been right. Everyone in the diner appeared to know her. The manager ushered them to a booth, handing a menu only to Alice, while the waitress came by with Mrs. Bloom's coffee.

"They take such good care of me here," Mrs. Bloom explained as she tucked the napkin into her ever so slightly frayed blouse.

"What are you having, Mrs. Bloom?" Alice asked. "Oh, Jenny knows," Mrs. Bloom answered nodding to the waitress. "Order what you want, dear," this to Alice.

Not wanting to get buried in a menu, Alice ordered a BLT and coffee and waited to ask her question.

"So, how are you doing?" Mrs. Bloom asked.

"Reasonably well," Alice answered, leaving out how her grief was much greater than expected.

"And your brother?"

"He's fine too. Thanks. Your kids?" and so on until their orders came.

Alice's eyes widened as the waitress arrived with Mrs. Bloom's cheeseburger, topped with thick slices of raw onion, and a large side of French fries.

"At my age, why worry?" Mrs. Bloom said as she reached for the ketchup and Alice laughed. It was so reassuring to see Mrs. Bloom eat with relish. Rich had been wrong. This was not about death and dying.

"You know I can't get your remark out of my head," Alice said.

"What remark?"

"Oh, about Mother taking Dad so seriously. And that he was, 'you know.'"

"Well, he was," Mrs. Bloom said with a slight giggle.

A ripple of discomfort went through Alice. "Was what?"

"Oh, I don't know the word you would use nowadays, but Mr. Bloom and I used to get quite a kick out of watching some of your father's antics. He was so sensitive. A difficult man your father, but then you know that."

Alice suddenly wanted one of Mrs. Bloom's now ketchup-slathered fries. Instead she bit into her own pickle.

"Did I tell you about the time your father threw an enormous party and didn't invite Mr. Bloom and me just to get back at us?" Mrs. Bloom asked. "We certainly had a good laugh at that one."

Alice wasn't prepared to laugh. It was one thing to have fought her father her whole life, one thing to have railed against his dictums, but to know that his friends had laughed at him behind his back? Well, that was something else altogether. "Get back at you for what?" she asked, dis-ease taking over.

"Why it must have been the summer you were born, when we rented houses next door to each other on the lake. We watched those trucks pull up, and the tables come out, and the chairs, and the food. Truckloads your father ordered. Just because he thought we'd invited our mutual landlady to lunch without him."

"Had you?" Alice asked, even though she knew it was beside the point.

"No. The landlady stopped by to check on something or other. We were about to sit down for lunch, so we invited her to stay. Well, your father saw us all eating together on our porch and got so furious that he'd been excluded, he wouldn't speak to us for weeks. He wouldn't let your mother talk to us either. Of course the minute he drove back to the city on Monday morning, your mom ran over to apologize for his behavior. The moment his car was in the driveway on Friday night, she'd become incommunicado again."

"How did it resolve itself?"

"Who can remember? Somehow it always did with your father. Usually he'd forget why he was angry and just pick up where we left off, as if nothing had happened."

Any hope Alice had Mrs. Bloom's memory was faulty, or that she was exaggerating, disappeared with those words. She'd described his behavior exactly as Alice knew it to be.

"Your poor mother, what she put up with."

Alice's half-eaten sandwich remained on the plate. Her fingers playing with the handle of the coffee mug. "Why do you think she did?" she asked, not certain she wanted the answer.

"Because she was so grateful to him for marrying her," Mrs. Bloom said, as if it should have been obvious. Then, noting Alice's look of surprise, added, "Why Alice, you must have known that for most of her life your mother didn't think she was attractive," this as Jenny refilled both women's coffee and Mrs. Bloom poured more cream into hers.

Alice was stunned. Her mother, who spent so much time on her looks, thought of herself as unattractive? It didn't make sense. All that time in front of the mirror, not out of vanity but to gain approval?

"Alice?"

"Oh, sorry, Mrs. Bloom, I was just trying to put it all together."

"Well, Alice, your father was gorgeous, and your mother was so grateful he married her that she lived her life saying thank you. You can't be on equal footing if you keep having to say thank you, now can you?" Then Mrs. Bloom ordered a piece of apple pie and ice cream. Alice declined dessert.

"Where were you so long?" Bill asked as she walked in. "It's after four." He had offered to stay with her after her mom died and didn't appear to be moving out.

"I walked most of the way home."

"From West End?" He closed his laptop and put some papers away in a drawer. "Watch it," a friend of her mother's had once said. "If you don't learn to live with someone soon, even a toothbrush will take up too much room."

Alice kicked off her shoes and tossed her two large shopping bags into the bedroom. "You must have really gotten into something deep or you wouldn't have trekked all the way home."

She was surprised at how well he was getting to know her.

"So? What did you two discuss?"

"Tell you later. Right now I need a bath. I'm exhausted."

Alice took off her clothes and went into the bathroom. She ran the water and stared for a minute at the full-length mirror. Her body wasn't bad. Better than she remembered her mother's at the same age. She could do something with her hair. Have it shaped. Maybe a bit of color to cover the grey.

She sank into the tub allowing the hot water to run over her feet. She'd meant to catch the bus home, but after depositing Mrs. Bloom at her door, Alice found herself walking across the park, passing the familiar landmarks of her youth as she tried to sort herself from her mother, her mother from herself. She hadn't realized how far she'd walked until she found herself, almost an hour later, at 39th and Fifth directly in front of Lord & Taylor's. Not able to resist, she walked in, wandering the main floor before stopping at the Clinique counter her mother's "You know dear, you really are vain," replayed as Alice tried on some lipstick. "Me?" Alice had said, stifling a roar at the absurdity of the remark. "You're the one always primping."

And suddenly Alice understood her mother's words from so long ago: "Oh, but my dear, I know I need to."

Alice couldn't believe how she'd missed the obvious. That all her mother's hours in front of a mirror had nothing to do with self-absorption–simply a way to guarantee her husband's interest. And here Alice had spent her life refusing to do anything with herself just to spite them both. Even her choice of men was in reaction to her father's constant intrusions. Men in whose visual apathy she had found a haven. What had her first therapist said? Rebels are attached to that which they rebel against? Well, her mother hadn't been the only one to take her father so seriously, now had she?

"How long are you going to be in there?" Bill called into her.

"Almost ready. Pour me a glass of wine, will you?"

Alice got out of the tub and wrapped herself in a towel. She brushed her hair back off her face, touched up the makeup the cosmetics lady had applied, and then reached into the Lord & Taylor bag, taking out her new full-length silk robe, with its long kimono-like sleeves and tassled sash. She tore off the price tag–no need for Bill to see it, as her mother would say. Then she went in, wondering if he would notice. Not that it mattered, really.

The Last Rumba

It was not a tragedy. Tragedies, by definition, involve someone larger than life brought down by a major character flaw. Or innocents felled by horrific events. Then again, isn't anyone we care about deeply larger than life? And don't we all have character flaws? Besides, if it was not a tragedy, then what the hell was it? Lord knows, there was plenty of destruction wreaked upon the innocent. Still, to label it one huge waste of a life is so banal that in itself makes it tragic. At least that's how it seems.

So, where to start? At the end? None of our lives truly end with death, especially if those who are left behind continue to respond to the deceased, as if the person is still present, still inflicting his will. And, as for the beginning, well, beginnings are so arbitrary aren't they? I mean where do our stories actually start? With us? Or those who came before? Or the ones who came before them? None of us starts with a clean slate, now do we?

What I can't do is let Richard tell the tale. Not because he died–that's never a problem for a storyteller–or because I wish to remain in control. I have no desire to make this my story. It's just that for most of his life, my brother Richard refused even the slightest of insights. Only when all his toys were gone, all escape hatches closed, did he have moments of resounding awareness—recoiling as quickly from those like bare feet on hot coals, fearful they would sear away protective layers of skin.

But I will not judge. I, by profession, know how difficult it is to accept uncomfortable truths. So if there are judgments to be made, I will leave them to you. What else can one do when the person you once adored, exhibits so much of what you loathe? Someone you still run to the moment he calls, and someone who can turn you into a stunned, ashamed bystander the moment you arrive.

Perhaps the best thing to do is to toss the proverbial dice–he would like that–and see on which moments in time they land. Some I witnessed. Some I played a part in. And some I can only imagine.

We move to the Latin beat, knees manipulating hips, our movements tight, controlled. It is our language. He transforming rage, pain, liquor into charismatic showmanship; me, enticing onlookers to watch as I lose myself in the music.

Eastchester Community Hospital: Room 457

I glance up from my book to find Richard's eyes on me. I move mine back to the page. I have no desire to get any more locked in than I am. I wonder what he's thinking. If he even is thinking. As for myself, I attempt rational thought, but most of my normal powers of reason have been superseded by emotion. I've become the perfect Pavlovian reacting to commands on cue: "Water!" "Here!" "Get my nurse!" "She's on her way." "I'm cold!" "I'll get more blankets." "I'm hot!" "I'll get some ice." "I need you!" "I'm coming." "Leave!" "I'm going."

As thin as he is, he's no way as emaciated as our mother was. His bones have flesh hanging from them. Not like hers jutting out through translucent parchment and transforming her face so it no longer resembled the woman we knew. Those eyes! Had they seen him? Who could tell?

After she died, he ran around telling everyone how his mother–suddenly she was only his–had known he was there. Bragged how she recognized him, knew it was him next to her as they said their goodbyes. This after months of finding every possible excuse to stay away, convinced it was unnecessary to visit because her mind was gone. "C'mon, Alice. It's been blown to bits." No, I'd tell him, if you stay longer, you'll see. But try convincing someone who wants out to come in. It took staying power to catch our mother's moments of clarity; her startling pronouncements which would emerge without warning. "Your father's oatmeal was better. . ." "Did you return the robe? . . ." "What happened to my breasts? My beautiful breasts? They're gone."

He never heard those words, never got to see her eat with relish the spoonfuls of mush that sustained her. Never caught her giggle at something the nurse said. And, never heard her whispered "forever" to my "I love you."

His choice. His loss. He could have come when told all food had been waved away and she'd said enough even to water. But that's how he lived his life. A star in a cameo role. The screen lights up, the excitement builds. He's home! "Dance with me." "Put your feet on my shoes." "I'm dancing!" "Yes." "More!" "Later." "Please!" "Not now!" "What are you doing?" "Stuff." "What stuff?" "None of your business." And he's gone. Fade to black.

A nurse enters and I'm waved out of the room. It's ridiculous really. I've seen everything there is to see. Tubes down his throat, catheter in his penis, urine in the bag. I watch him disintegrate just as I watched the others–they who invaded my privacy and who years later were required by age and need to relinquish theirs to me.

Oh Richard. In spite of all you do, I love you. In spite of who you've become. In spite. I admit to feeling spiteful. The better he gets, the more spiteful I become. True, during the height of the crisis I panicked into helplessness. A puppet pulled in whatever direction his emotions took me. But now that it seems he'll get better, at least for a time, I find myself shooting silent barbs like quills from a porcupine. You did this to yourself. . . No one else, you! No matter. My anger cannot compare with his volcanic rage.

I'm well aware it's trite to describe rage as "volcanic," but it's the only adjective that works. I know. I've been looking up words in the dictionary since I was nine when Richard decided we should learn ten new words a day starting with the A's. Naturally, within a day or two he grew bored. But I remained hooked. Not that I stayed with the original plan or found many opportunities to use most of the words before they disappeared from my head. But volcanic? That one I've looked up so many times. Volcanos: active, dormant or extinct. Four main forms or phases of eruption–Hawaiian, Strombolian, Vulcanian and Peleean–which may or may not occur within one volcano. The last named for Mt. Pelee which erupted in 1902 (coincidentally, the year our father arrived from Russia) and managed to annihilate all those in its path except for two: a convict and a young girl. I find that particularly ironic.

Richard has never been dormant. Not even when asleep or dozing off. Gas forms, lava simmers, heat bubbles up, warning those too close he may blow at any moment, in any direction. Even during those weeks on the respirator, unable to do more than motion with his hands, grimace with his face and scribble illegibly on a board, he sputtered and spit somewhere between Hawaii and Stromboli. I do not relish his getting better.

The nurse calls me back into the room. She ignores him, less tied up in the drama of it all. I return to the chair and pick up my book. It's a Brookner that failed. What better place than a room where I have to be, need to be and do not wish to be, to force myself through the pile of books I keep putting down out of sheer boredom.

My brother speaks. "I can't remember Dad smiling," he says, as if for the first time. As if I haven't heard it before. "I know this is going to sound silly, but. . ." "Can you think of a time when Dad. . .?" It's not dementia. Just the ability to dig past the question to what lies beneath was never his strong-point.

"Except once," he says. "Once he let loose. Can't remember the occasion, but he had one too many. The rest of the time . . . All I can see is that look of disapproval."

Richard's one up on me. I can't remember a single let loose. Can't even imagine one occurring. But a smile if that's what one would call the eyes lit and a small upward curl of the lips, that smile I know. Our father's way of seducing all with an offer of food, drink, or a re-instatement of existence. Seduction: deflection's perfect tool.

"Dad certainly smiled that last Mother's Day," I say. "Don't you remember? He ran around the room giving everyone kisses. Oh, God! And a rose. He gave each of us a rose."

"Wasn't there."

"Oh, yes, yes you were."

"Well, I don't remember anything like that."

"C'mon, Richard. Dad was in his bathrobe and slippers. In the den. We were all sitting around in a circle. It was so shocking. All that energy from someone who hadn't eaten or gotten out of bed in days. Mania I guess. For God's sake, how could you forget? He went to bed right after and four days later he was gone."

"Christ! Can't you ever leave the past?"

And you refuse to look at it, I want to say.

"What time is it?" he demands. It's become a fixation.

"Six-twenty."

"They're late with dinner."

"It should be here soon."

"It should be here now," he roars in good old Strombolian fashion.

"Maybe it means you're getting better. Certainly looks as if they're not as concerned."

My attempt to present him with other ways to deal with frustration goes unnoticed.

"Go see where it is!" he demands.

"I'm sure it will be here in a moment," I tell him.

"Go Goddamn it!"

Which I do. I actually get up, walk to the door and of course run smack into the aide coming in with the tray. The epitome of the current crop of hospital caretakers, she shoves the tray on the bed table and leaves without a word. I silence my "I told you so" and start to arrange the tray.

"What are you doing?" he snaps.

"Removing the lids."

"Did I ask you to?"

I give up.

"Then do it yourself, Rich,"

"I will."

"Fine." I return to my chair and Brookner.

"Goddamn them" he roars.

"Now what?"

"It's not what I ordered."

"You sure are your father's son."

"What the hell do you mean by that?"

He knows exactly what I mean. In our father's eyes, all food was meant to be sent back at least once, often ruined in the process, just to prove he was knowledgeable, demanding, a connoisseur.

Richard waves the menu at me as if to separate himself from our father. "Look! Look! I wrote down no gravy. I spent a whole hour on the phone with the dietician. Do they listen? No!" His voice gets louder and louder until the rasping peaks. "I said 'no gravy' and they've drowned it."

"Push it to the side," I whisper.

"I shouldn't have to!"

I imagine his voice carrying out into the hall, past the nurses' station, into the rooms where people lie in various stages of sickness and dying. I get up to leave.

"Where the hell are you going?"

"To heat up the soup I brought."

"When I want soup, I'll ask."

"I think I'll head home," I say.

"No one asked you to stay."

"If I leave now I can get the express train."

"So go!"

"I'll be here in the morning. I have patients in the afternoon."

"You don't have to come at all."

"Tomorrow morning," I repeat and pick up my coat as he tears his teeth into a roll. In a few seconds he will have indigestion. I don't bother to warn the nurses. They probably already know. Still, I am leaving of my own volition. A definite improvement.

Cugat blasts and everyone else moves aside. We are center stage. There is a pause in the music and he turns away to give another woman her chance. I am alone on the floor. No man joins me, the wives forbid it.
Same

He knows he shouldn't have yelled. But he has to yell at someone. The nurses aren't listening. His doctors don't give a shit. No one understands how horrific this is. He can't even take a piss without someone coming in to check it.

He hates that Alice pities him. Doesn't want her pity. Doesn't want anyone's pity. Just wants the hell out, one way or another. Besides, either way, it's feet first. Now that's funny enough to pass on. He'll tell Gail: Black bag or walking, it's feet first. She'll laugh.

"Hey," he says to the nurse with big boobs. He likes big boobs. He wants to reach out and grab them. "I got an idea for a new laxative. It's called Scared Shit of Dying. What do you think? Want to market it with me? We could make a fortune." Big boobs has no sense of humor.

He reaches for the phone and dials. No answer. Without thinking he leaves Gail a message. He shouldn't have. Now he can't call again or she'll think he's checking up on her. Maybe she'll call him before they switch off the incoming lines. If not, he's stuck with only the nurses to talk to and they're sick of him. Not one of them gives a damn if he sticks around.

New York Presbyterian Hospital: A semi-private room.

Hospitals scare him, yet here he is. Six o'clock in the morning. Sitting in a chair across from me. His eyes red. I ordered him to come, but still. . .

"I'm frightened, Rich."

"Me too."

We both think: Helen.

"You'll stay, yes?"

"I'll be here when they bring you down."

"Promise?"

"Promise."

"Love you."

"Love you too."

At Home: mine.

I missed the express and got stuck waiting for the local–shivered on the platform like an animal emerging from a pool of muddy water, attempting to shake off the silt and scum. It's okay. I need time for re-entry. I don't know what I pray for so I don't pray. Don't actually believe in it. Prayer has never curtailed death. It's a placebo—seventeen percent palliative.

The answering machine is blinking. There's always one patient who requires attention. Sometimes they call and don't leave a message–the sound of my voice sufficient to tide them over until the next session. I never phoned my therapist unless it was to change an appointment, yet I've never stopped patients from calling me. There are five messages: two from patients, one from Norma, a hang-up, and Gail. Every night his mistress calls. Actually the ex-mistress. No, not even actually. Gail is no mistress. She's never been kept. She simply was involved with Richard over a period of years. Therefore, Gail is one of many women who entered into an affair with Richard–either for one-night or longer–all of whom helped him maintain the status quo of a wife, two children, a dog and a house in the suburbs. In other words, Gail is a masochist. Anyone who stays involved with Richard is a masochist. A sister, by duty, blood and circumstance, is exempt.

On the train, I tried to imagine our father letting loose. Couldn't. For that matter, I couldn't conjure him up at all. Of course, just because neither Richard nor I can remember our father laughing, does not mean he never laughed. I know not to trust memory. Mine. My patients'. Richard's. Especially Richard's. He can never understand why I keep our family history, its mementos, why I don't ditch the entire past.

"Why do you want all that crap?"

"Because, it's our history."

"Their history. Not yours. Not mine."

"Ours, Richard. Ours."

"Christ. You know, for a shrink, you're crazy."

I poor a glass of wine, go to the bookshelf, and remove our family album—yellow pictures, however faded, can undo the corruption of memory. I start leafing through. And there's the proof. Our father rolling in the sand, legs entwined around one of our uncles, both men in 1930's black bathing suits, chest and thighs covered, grinning at the camera. I could bring it to Rich. But for what purpose? It was before I was born. Maybe before he was born. Besides, the one right next to it contradicts it entirely. Another uncle and our dad: two peacocks on the boardwalk with walking sticks and three piece suits—the fashion of the day. Of the two, our father cuts the more elegant figure. His brother, our uncle, shorter, stockier, places himself a few steps closer to the lens: the acknowledged patriarch, rival, success. Which boardwalk? Atlantic City? Atlantic Beach? One and the same. A place to go in those days. A place to be seen. A place to report back that you've been. As for the women, most likely they are taking the picture, standing off to the side—beautifully outfitted, simply not as important. He certainly was a looker, our father.

The phone rings. It's Richard. As long as I'm coming in the morning, he wants a bagel. Really fresh. Poppy. Nothing on it. And a decent cup of coffee. Maybe I could pick up a thermos. Oh, and a piece of fruit like a plum or a peach. But only if it's good.

"Do you want me to bring lunch?" I ask.

"How the hell do I know now what I'll want for lunch?" conveniently forgetting it's easier for me to pick up food around the corner than near the hospital. Not to mention if he wants anything from the hospital menu, he has to do so a day in advance.

"See you in the morning," I say. I hate my passivity. I dial him back but the operator won't put me through. Incoming calls to patients are not accepted after 8:30.

Room 457 9:40a.m.

He knows Alice thinks it's his own fault he's here. He made his bed so he can damn well lie in it. Well, fuck her. With all her degrees, she knows nothing. There are plenty of people who did everything right and they're in just as bad shape as he is. Some even worse.

He presses the buzzer for the nurse. A voice comes over the speaker. It sounds like a recording.

"Can I help you?"

"I want to walk around."

"I'll come when I finish here."

"I want to walk now."

"You'll have to wait."

"Can't you understand what this is like?"

He'll be damned if he'll wait. He pulls himself up and yanks the oxygen plugs from his nose. If she doesn't get in here in a few seconds, he's walking out on his own. He reaches for his robe on the end of the bed and manages to put it on. His feet find his slippers. He stands up, gets dizzy and falls. . .

I walk in. Two nurses are struggling to maneuver Richard back into bed. He's crying. They order me to leave. I back out. There's blood on the floor. I lean against the wall outside the door and choke back unexpected sobs. The bag with bagels dangling from my hand.

"He'll be all right," another nurse assures. "His skin is thin. It bleeds easily. He'll be okay."

"For how long?" I whisper.

The nurse shrugs. "Go in," she says.

I don't want to. I want to leave and never come back. What the hell am I doing coming here day after day? I want someone to take me away. Anywhere.

I walk in. "Hi," I say.

He's not talking.

"I brought you the bagel and some fruit. Didn't have a thermos, so no coffee. I can go downstairs to the cafeteria, but I don't think it'll be much better than what they have on the floor."

More silence.

"Do you want me to put it out for you?"

His fingers tighten. They used to curl into a fist. They can't anymore.

"I thought I'd stay about an hour and then head back. My first patient is at 1:30."

It's going to be one of those visits. If I speak, he will rage in silence. If I remain silent, he will sink into depression and his despair will overwhelm us both.

I sit and reach for a book. I've brought two today. The Brookner I'll never finish—even though it's only 187 pages—and Jamieson's on manic depression. There are others I'd prefer to read, but have left them at home. They all have death or dying in the title.

I try again.

"Rich, you've got to eat something." With that the room erupts.

"I don't want to eat. I don't want to talk. I just want to be left alone. Do you understand? I don't want you here. I don't want anyone here. Do you hear me?"

"Everyone can hear you."

"Good. Then just sit there and say nothing."

If a patient pulled that, I'd let out a guffaw. Okay, maybe I'd be slightly more contained, but it would be damn clear I found it amusing. Instead, I sit and say nothing. Our father was a master at silence and now I am our father's daughter. I go back to my book.

"Can you stay for lunch?" I hear Richard ask.

I actually consider cancelling a patient. The moment passes.

"Richard, I told you. I have appointments." Then, without thinking out comes, "What the hell do you think is paying your rent?"

Eastchester Hospital. Room 457

Just like Alice, the shrink wants him to talk. Every day he comes, sits by his bed and waits for a gut spill. But what's there to say? That he doesn't want to die? Who does? That he's made mistakes? Who hasn't? Besides, it's not going to change a Goddamn thing. It's not going to put money in the bank. It's not going to get him back on the road. Life is what it is. Try telling that to Alice. She talked to a shrink non-stop for years and what has it done for her? Does she have someone to fuck? No, she's like a rag, mopping up after everybody. And so what if his father wouldn't let him take over, gave it to an employee? How does rehashing shit help a thing? Help him get out of this bed? Anyone want to tell him that? Anyone?

Home: mine

The phone rings. I don't have to reach for it. I've gotten into the habit of sleeping with it on my bed, my hand on the receiver. I sleep–if you can call it that–as if listening to a newborn's breathing in the next room. Not until dawn, when the light from the window crosses my face, do I finally fall off from exhaustion. I've begun to rely on an alarm to wake me. I've no idea where I am.

"They're talking hospice," the voice says.

"What?"

"They're talking hospice."

I'm wide awake.

"Who's talking hospice?"

"The doctors for Christ's sake! They're talking hospice."

I choke up. I have wished him gone for so long and still I choke up. Why aren't I relieved? "It doesn't make sense," I say, even though some part of me knows it makes perfect sense. How many transfusions can one consume to stay alive?

"You know what hospice is, right?" his voice weak, frightened. It's scary as hell.

"Of course I know," I say. "What caused them to switch like this?"

"Nothing. They came in this morning and said hospice. They said it wouldn't hurt. They'd give me plenty of morphine."

"Can you get the doctors together, Rich? I can be up there by five-thirty. Can you get them together so we can all talk?"

"I'll try," he whispers, his voice shaking. There's no argument. No fight.

"Do it, Richard. Get them together."

He says he will and then, "Alice?"

"What?"

"Nothing."

"Rich, you're not going so fast. Do you hear me? You're not."

I'm more frightened than I've ever been.

Eastchester Hospital. Same Room

In stark contrast to the subject under discussion, the doctors are a study in casual. One slumps against the wall. Another against a chair. The head doctor has positioned himself closest to the patient, his arms resting on the railing of the bed guard, his hands proprietarily draped over Richard's body. Only the one female doctor gives a clue to the underlying tension. She stands near the door, folded in on herself, a chart clasped across her chest. Richard has made it clear I'm to be an equal participant so I choose my spot with care: in front of the window where I have a good view of their faces. Richard has gathered them all: Hematology, Urology, Oncology, Cardiology. Not the action of someone ready to die.

"Why did you suggest hospice?" I ask.

"We were just responding to Richard's saying he'd had enough." the head man says. He oozes ego.

My spine straightens in protest. "He said he'd had enough before and you always talked him out of it."

The female doctor steps in: "Alice, you know the last few months have been hell on him. There comes a point when if the patient doesn't want to fight, we have to go along. Not to mention he's been fighting this on and off for over ten years now."

My: "I am more than aware the length of time and it's Dr. Wallach not Alice," remains unsaid. "If it were you, would you give up?" I ask the head guy, his hands now in his pockets. It's the same question I ask my vet. "If it were your animal, what would you do?" My vet tells me; this doc doesn't.

"Who knows until we get there, right?" he parries. "All we know is there's no guarantee if we keep going much is going to change. It could, but we can't promise." This from the doctor who swore when Richard begged to be taken off the respirator, that he could pull him through. "Won't be easy," he'd said. "But I can bring you back and get you breathing on your own." What Richard hadn't asked, was physically incapable of asking–if the thought even entered his mind– was "Back to what?" It had crossed my mind, standing next to the respirator, looking at Richard's excruciatingly thin, bruised body, tubes in every orifice. Oh how I'd wanted this self-proclaimed miracle worker to tell me just what he was bringing Richard back to. But I kept my mouth shut, afraid Richard might think my question implied I wanted him dead. Now here we were, reaping the rewards of what long ago I'd labeled Ego-Driven Medical Procedures, having the discussion we should have had months ago.

Richard's voice startles us all. "What are my odds?"

"What?" The doctors respond almost in unison

"If we continue, what are my odds?"

The doctors pause, turn toward each other and conference, seemingly oblivious to the patient and family member in the room. As if the recitation of statistics could have no impact on the patient's will to fight. Each comes up with his or her own estimate based on their particular specialty. The figures vary from a survival rate of 75 to 40 percent the first year to 60 to 30 the next and downhill from there. Throughout the exchange my eyes remain fixed on Richard. The numbers have found their mark–his mortality is hitting home.

"I think we need some time to digest all of this," I say and the doctors, obviously relieved at the escape hatch I've offered, nod, say their "sleep well's," a directive or two to the nurses, and exit, en masse.

Still Room 437

He calls everybody: Gail, the consulting physician, his friend Dave. (He doesn't call Billy. Rich has a good idea what his kid thinks.) He even calls the hospital shrink. He says, more or less, the same thing to all of them. "Docs gave me a choice: hospice or more of the same shit. If I can hang in, maybe they'll find a cure, either way, money would be tight, might need help." He ends each call with a "So what do you think?"

His shrink answers as shrinks answer: "What do you think?"

Gail bursts into tears. She's been expecting him to die for a year now and yet she gets all emotional as if the thought has never entered her mind. Go figure.

The consulting physician says to stick it out a bit longer. Of course he'd say that. He gets paid for his consultations.

And Dave is at a loss. "Jesus, Rich, this has to be your decision," is all he can come up with.

The last call is to Alice. She says if he didn't want to live, he wouldn't be asking everyone what to do. She adds something about not being ready to turn her home into a hospice. At least that's what he thinks she says. Getting fuzzy. Or was he dreaming. He's not sure.

Ten years earlier at my therapist's office.

"He won't see me."

"Who?"

"Rich. He won't let me in to see him. He sees everyone else, but not me."

"Why do you need him to see you?"

"Because I'm his sister! And he's sick. Besides, what will everyone say?"

"And why do you care what others say?"

But that's my story. Not his. So we'll skip it.

Another train ride. Coming? Going?

I published a paper putting forth the theory that incest does not have to be the sexual act carried to completion for it to exist. Of course, displaced sexuality would have been the far appropriate term for both of us. He did after all screw everything in sight. Starting with my sitter when I was two, right through to Gail, or whoever was his last bed spring. My sexual encounters less frequent, sporadic, never long-lasting. Same thing really. Both of us thoroughly screwed up. Thoroughly screwed out. Thoroughly screwed. And now, here he lies. Making sexual advances to nurses. Telling jokes about the sex act. Justifying his behavior with stories of other men maintaining virile thoughts right to their end. His version of intimacy. I wonder if he ever was any good in bed. I can't imagine he would be. No patience. No ability to care for anyone else. Counting on his endowment to do the work for him. It's what one of his lovers told me. The one who left him for a woman. He thinks his penis will turn me straight." Do most men think like that? Certainly plenty of my male patients do–straight or gay. It's all in the penis.

I only had one patient like him, and he didn't stay more than a few visits. I often wonder what happened to him, thinking, albeit irrationally, if I knew how he turned out, I would know Richard's fate. Maybe even understand how Rich came to be. Not that any two people are alike or any history the same. Certainly not mine and Richard's. We were like two cats I once had from the same litter. One hid at the sight of the vacuum; the other chased it around the room as if it were a beast to be slain. I should have gone into family therapy. Maybe then I could have helped him. Study the same scenes from different perspectives.

Room 457
"Did you talk about me?"
"When?"
"When you were in therapy? What did you talk about when you were in therapy?"
"Are you thinking about therapy?"
"Christ! Can't you just answer a question?"
"I talked about whatever was on my mind. Sometimes the past, sometimes the present, usually the relationship between the two."
"Self-indulgent bullshit!"
"On some level, you might be right. I repeat, are you thinking of talking to someone?" I manage to omit, "finally."
"They've had someone coming by."
"And?"
"And what?"
"Has it helped?"
"We talk, but then I run out of things to say. Anyway, what's it going to change?"

"Maybe nothing. Maybe it will help you get through whatever is coming. Put things in order."

"You don't think I'm going to make it, do you?"

"I didn't say that."

"It's what you meant. 'Put things in order' means before I die."

"We're all going to die, Richard. I just meant it could help you understand what went on." What do I want from him? "Have you seen Billy?"

"The little shit hasn't come by."

I bite my tongue. What am I going to say? That he was never a father, so why should his son be a son? That he treated his son worse than his father treated him?

"Maybe you could call him. Just see how he's doing."

And of course he explodes. "You never let up do you?"

"Sorry. Just thought . . ."

Silence again. Then, "I was top of my class, you know."

"Yes."

"Maybe Mom shouldn't have skipped me."

"'What do you mean?"

"Maybe Mom shouldn't have kept skipping me ahead. Why did she do that?"

"Why do you think?"

He explodes again, "Goddamn it, you're playing shrink again."

"Sorry. Training. I think she liked the bragging rights." I wait. Will he connect the dots?

"Well, it put me with a much older crowd. I don't think it was good for me."

I don't respond.

"Well, I don't think it was."

I wait.

"Well, I don't."

I am debating whether to connect the dots for him.

"So?"

"So, what?" I ask.

"What do you think? You're the shrink."

"I think you made Dad jealous, going off to college so young," and hold my breath for another explosion, but shockingly none comes. There's nothing but silence as the thought penetrates. I can see he's starting to put the pieces together, but then he stops.

"You're always blaming them," he says.

"No, I don't blame them. I'm just saying what was. They had their own history. We have ours."

He doesn't want to hear any more and I leave it alone. What good would it do anyway? Allow him to die in peace? Doubtful.

We move to the Latin beat, knees manipulating hips, the movements small, tight, highly controlled. Our last dance. He's not breathing well. We stand in place and sway. It's enough.

PART TWO

And other stories

At The Algonquin

At The Algonquin

"You know why their relationship is doomed?" Jim says, as his hand takes ownership of my thigh.

"No, why?" I ask. I want to know about doomed relationships.

"Well, it's obvious," he says. "I mean, can you imagine finding out about someone only after the ring is on?"

"Pete must have known something about her," I tell him as he pours himself a scotch from the small bottle into a plastic cup.

"Nah," he says. "Pete had it in his head that he had to have a tall blonde and Gillian was so panicked she'd be a spinster, she just became whatever he wanted. Now look at them. You can see him looking over at her wondering who the hell she is. Not like you. You laid all your cards out on the table right from the beginning. Told me who you were and who you weren't. And you sure have been true to your word which is why each day it just . . ."

"Providence!" the conductor yells so I miss the end of Jim's thought. Doesn't matter. I know what he's going to say: ". . . it just gets better and better." He says it almost daily. I hand him my bottle of wine.

"What did you do before you had me to open things for you?" he jokes. I smile and play with the diamond heart he's chained around my neck. "Well, aren't you going to say something?" he says. "Like, it gets better for you too?"

"If you have to ask. . ." I say, still smiling.

I count. There are seven men lined up waiting to exit the train all talking into their cell phones at once. Don would have turned it into a contrapuntal piece for male voices.

Tenor: "Hi honey, we're pulling in. Where will you be waiting?"

Bass enters softly, slowly building through the next six bars: "Pulling in … Pulling in … Pulling in." Baritone (forte) "Did you pick up the kids? (Beat) You're kidding." Second baritone: "What's for dinner?" Tenor: "What's for dinner?" Bass: "What's for dinner?" Tenor (mournfully): "No! I-didn't-get-the-job." Rest, 2, 3, 4. All together: "Oh! No! Not meat loaf again!!!"

The train stops. The doors open. The men exit.

I can see Don at the piano poised somewhere between a seated and standing position as the back of his leg pushes away the piano bench. His hands leave the keys, their long fingers eloquently gesturing each singers' entrance as if were reaching down into them to draw out the sound. That's what he did to me. Reached down and drew out my soul. All of it.

Two men get on followed by a woman with a tote bag slung around her neck; a large, heavy suitcase that she's trying to maneuver in front of her with one hand; and a child in tow with the other. You can tell the kid is shy and clingy. Or maybe the mother is over-protective. Or both. The woman's got to be in her late forties. Looks tired. Tense. Probably a single working mom. Typical! With all the seats to choose from, she takes the two directly in front of us. At least the kid doesn't seem the type to demand everyone's attention. Sort of mousey. Pray she's not a whiner. The woman looks down at me and smiles. I forget that I've been smiling and drop my mouth to neutral. Mothers with kids are not my thing.

"Six months I give them," Jim continues. He tends to stay on a subject until there's nothing left of it. "Six months, then you and I will have to go there and pick up the pieces."

He's already thinking that far ahead. I can't. Have been going at this day by day. Trying not to plan. I haven't even thought about what's going to happen when we get to Philly and meet his kids. He swears they'll like me. That I'll like them, too. Well, maybe I will. Maybe I won't. I've decided it's not important. What will be, will be. They're grown. We're grown. What's the difference?

I watch Jim spill the packet of pretzels onto his tray, the veins in his hands beginning to show. But then, so are mine. I take my fingers off the heart and fold them over my ring. He hasn't asked that I replace it. I wouldn't even if he did. Couldn't. He knows that, I think.

"If all Pete wants is a tall blonde," I say, "who cares who or what Gillian is? He got what he wished for, right?" I can't remember if that's a lyric from a song or just sounds like one. I'm slipping. Used to carry on entire conversations with Don using only the lyrics. I haven't told Jim this. He'd want to try.

"C'mon on," he says. "You can't mean that. She cooked for him, went hiking with him. Now suddenly she wants to eat out all the time and finds every excuse imaginable to stay in town. You heard him. He might have been making light of it, but he knows she's not who he thought she was. Listen," Jim says, as if I weren't. "I've got to make some calls. I'll go stand in the corridor so you can read."

He's considerate to a fault. Don wasn't. But then, they're apples and oranges, which is exactly what I wanted. No comparing. So I say, "Don't be silly. Stay here. I'm okay, really." And I am. Certainly better than I've been in a long time. The tears have stopped. I've put the weight back on. I'm exercising again. I really am okay. Life is what it is.

The woman in front of us has deposited the kid on the seat by the window and is straining to put the suitcase on the rack. I nudge Jim to help. He's up in a flash. "Hold on a second, Frank," he says into the phone, then hands it to me while he flings her bag over our heads, takes the phone back, and continues talking without missing a beat. It's one of the things that attracted me to him. His ability to take over everyone and everything including me.

"Thanks," the woman says, smiling up at him. Jim makes a face indicating to her that it was nothing, and motions to me that he's going to continue his conversation up front where it's more private. He's tall–6'2". Don swore he was 5'10", Truth was he was a good inch shorter.

The woman pulls out a book for her daughter and continues to stand, smiling. I can see she's about to say something. I look down. The last thing I need is for her to ask me to babysit so she can get something to drink. Definitely she's a working mom. They're easy to spot. It's the makeup that gives them away. Stay-at-home moms get out of the habit of wearing makeup. When they do put it on, it's either too much or so sparing that it looks half done. Working moms are practiced. They can hit it right on. No thinking twice. A finished look in three minutes flat.

I can feel her still staring at me. I glance up. She smiles and continues fussing with her daughter. I look away again, but she can't resist. Bends down and in a voice all polite and hushed says, "Excuse me. I don't mean to be rude, but aren't you Janet Elder? I heard you sing one night years ago at the Algonquin in New York. You were really good!"

Now what am I supposed to do with that? Tell her I still am good? Or that I'm not who she thinks I am? Or that I was Janet Elder, it's just that Janet Elder doesn't exist anymore. That Janet Elder stopped being the day Don died. No, they already wrote that song. Best to cut it short. Say thank you and start reading. "Thanks," I say. "Glad you enjoyed."

I'm surprised she recognized me. Most people never remember cabaret singers. Or at least can't recognize them without the slinky black dress, high heels and rhinestones. Besides, my hair is completely changed. It used to be long and full. I could do all sorts of things with it. Put it up like Madame Pompadour or let it hang down like a demure Deana Durbin. Now it's cropped short. Can't imagine how she knew it was me.

"Do you still perform? I don't get out like I used to," she says and nods in the direction of her daughter, leaving me to fill in the blanks. I wonder if she makes the kid feel guilty for having been born.

"I haven't performed in a while," I tell her. "So you haven't missed anything. But thanks."

"Well, I hope you do again soon," she says. "I really enjoyed you. Her father did, too. We thought you were really good." Then she turns and disappears into her seat.

So, I was right about her being a single mom–the "her father" instead of "my husband" a dead giveaway. I wonder where she's going. Whether she's come from home or heading there. Vanity. Two minutes before I didn't even want a smile from her, but now that she's recognized me, I want to know all. When she heard me? Was Don on piano? What she remembers about the music?

We're getting close to New Haven. Don taught there. One whole semester. A course on the interplay of music and lyrics from opera to Broadway. Brought me up to demonstrate. Not that he needed me. He could have done it just as well on his own, but we wanted a weekend away and got the school to pay for it without knowing. We found a small B&B. Sat by a fire drinking hot chocolate. A regular Bing Crosby movie. Christ! We even roasted marshmallows.

I watch Jim up in front, gesturing in the air as if the person on the other end of the phone can see him. He's tried to explain the market to me, but it's over my head. Musicians are supposed to be good with numbers and in many ways I am. It's just that I don't care whether a stock is high or low, or a product is moving, or the economy is on an upswing. Though it doesn't seem to bother Jim whether or not I do. He's got business partners for that, he says. I'm to be cherished. Adored. He's finished with the call and heading back. I smile as he gets close.

"Sorry," he says.

"No problem," I reply. He has no idea of how often I sat silent while Don composed in his head next to me. That was something I never quite understood either. I need to see the notes. Oh, not all of them. Once I made a song mine, I could improvise with the best of them. But Don, well he could write out a piece for a whole orchestra, every instrument's line, as easily as if he were writing a friend a letter. It always amazed me, his talent.

I decide not to tell Jim what the woman said. He never saw me perform. He's listened to tapes. Said he really likes them. But I could tell he didn't get it- he's too literal and I was known for what wasn't sung. Don put it differently. Said I wrote my own lyric, one that I'd be thinking of while singing the lyricist's words.

I need to stretch. I tell Jim I'm going to get a snack. He says he'll go. I tell him, I need the walk and ask if there's anything he wants. "Another scotch," he says, pulling out his billfold.

"I've got it," I say, and reach for my purse.

"Don't forget we're having dinner with the kids," he says, his look one of fatherly concern.

"I know," I tell him. "I'll just get some more pretzels or something." I brush past his legs, which have extended themselves into the aisle. His shoes are the black shiny leather kind with tassels. Don lived in sneakers. Old ones. Took me ages to get him to break in a new pair.

Now, I have no idea what possesses me, but as I start to walk in the aisle, I turn and ask the woman if she wants me to bring her and the kid something, or better yet, if she wants to walk with me. Then I go and offer Jim's services as a baby sitter. "You wouldn't mind, dear, would you?" I say, and of course he says yes, and the woman is asking her daughter if she would mind, it would only be a minute, and the daughter looks as if she is going to start to bawl, but I quickly say, we'll bring you back some cookies, so she stops and I tell the kid to go sit next to Jim, and at first he looks at me a bit weird, then he leans over the seat and smiles at the kid, and before you know it she's climbing over and the woman is thanking Jim profusely, and I manage to cut her off before she goes and says something stupid like how exciting it is to have a chance to chat with the Janet Elder.

"Irene," she says, introducing herself as we head towards the bar car.

"Janet, but you know that." Then, just to make conversation: "Quite a train. Sort of sci-fi looking, isn't it?"

And she says, "Yeah, but it looks like it should go faster than it actually does."

Then we shut up and concentrate on walking without falling into someone's lap.

There's a line in the bar car. Mostly men in shirts, their ties probably in their brief cases, their jackets left on their seats.

"You wouldn't like to have a drink here, would you?" Irene says.

It's obvious she needs a break. So, I say, "Sure, why not?"

"I love my daughter," she says, with all the guilt of a single parent. "It's just that it's been a long week what with her being out of school, visiting my folks, and seeing all those people I grew up with, along with their husbands and kids. And I have no doubt she'll be safe with . . ."

She's clearly trying to categorize him.

"Jim," I say, there being no reason to resort to labels. I wonder if I made a mistake. If I should have come on my own. But then I figure, what's one drink? Besides, it'll be easy to cut it short. We both have someone waiting.

We stand leaning against the side of the car. When it's our turn, I ask her what she wants. "My treat," I tell her.

"Oh, I couldn't," she says.

"Sure you can. You paid to hear me at the Algonquin, right?"

"Well, in that case, I'll have some white wine, but I'm paying for the juice and cookies for my daughter."

"You're on," I say.

As the bartender, or whatever he's called on a train, starts to fill two cardboard boxes with our order, Irene decides to run back and tell Marilyn where she'll be so the kid won't worry. "Tell Jim, too," I say, and hand her the box that I've rearranged with the scotch, juice, cookies and chips.

"Be back in a sec," she says and I believe her. She's already taken off.

I take our box with the wine and a bag of pretzels and grab two empty stools. Jim hates sitting at a bar. Always wants to go straight to the table. Not like Don and me. We loved sitting on stools. Ate on them. Drank on them. I even sang from a stool, though my feet never could touch the floor. I used to have to lock my heels around the rod at the top. When we could finally afford it, we had one specially made so the rod would be at the right height and I could rest the ball of my foot on it, cross my legs and let forth.

Irene is back. "That was quick," I say.

"Jim's being a doll, listening to Marilyn read aloud from her book and even looking interested. He said to enjoy yourself, he's got more calls to make. Though, from the looks of it, Marilyn is going to monopolize him."

I don't let on that I can't imagine her kid talking to anyone.

"How far are you going?" she asks, twisting open her bottle.

"Philly," I tell her.

"Baltimore for us. Took the train because it's easier with a kid. I would have thought you two would have flown," she says.

"I don't fly," I tell her.

"Oh," she says. And then that damn look comes over her face. The one I've seen all too many times. The one with shame and guilt and horror written all over it. "Oh, My God," she says. "I'm so sorry. I just remembered. I don't know how I could have forgotten. Oh, I feel just terrible. I really put my foot in it, didn't I?"

"It's okay," I say. "Honest." Of course it's not. But she didn't mean anything by it and isn't that what you're supposed to say? That it's okay?

"That's why you haven't performed," she says, going for the rest of the leg. I put the smile back on. It's something I learned to do right after Don died. Put a smile on your face and the whole human race—now there's a lyric.

"So, what about you?" I ask her. "Got on at Providence right?" She looks relieved that I've changed the subject. Didn't go into the gruesome details. Small plane. Overloaded. Bad weather. Six months in the hospital for me who sat in the back seat. Don and the pilot gone. "Originally home. Baltimore's where we live now. Who would have thought?" she says.

I nod, though at what I can't be sure.

"You live in Boston now? You guys don't seem the type."

"We're not," I tell her. "Jim had some business there." What I don't tell her is that as long as Jim has his phone, his Blackberry, his computer and a scotch, he doesn't seem to mind where the hell we are. She looks as if she's trying to get inside my head. I move my eyes out the window.

"How did you two meet?" she asks.

"Through friends," I tell her. I find it interesting that she sees us as a couple. We could simply be friends. Even family. Distant relations. Then, in a single breath, she proceeds to tell me how she met her ex on a ski trip in Europe, how he followed her back to the States where she got pregnant, married–in that order, then she moves to London with him, has the baby, he turns abusive–really bad–she tries to leave, he takes her to court demanding custody, her parents can't or won't help–I can't quite make out that part–and the night before the court's decision is about to come down, after it has cost her whatever savings she has, he disappears, just like that, never to be seen or heard from again.

"Sometimes I'm afraid he'll appear without warning, which is why I moved to a city where he'd never expect me to be."

"Wow!" I say. "That's quite a story."

She turns red and apologizes for dumping on me.

"It's okay," I say again.

And she repeats, "No, no it isn't. You've got your own stuff." Her face has gotten all tight and pinched like a lift job gone bad. She continues to apologize. "It's just that it's been a rough week what with listening to the women I went to school with telling me how great their lives are with their fabulous husbands, wonderful kids and expensive country clubs."

"You sure you don't want something stronger?" I ask.

"No," she says. "Wine is fine." Then, after an uncomfortable silence, she says, "Maybe I should be getting back."

"Listen," I say, a habit I must have picked up from Jim, this starting a sentence with "listen." "There's plenty of time. We're not even at Stamford yet. So tell me about the night you heard me sing."

Her face relaxes, but instead of talking about that night she says how nice it must be to have someone who takes care of you. "He does, doesn't he?" she asks. "Take care of you?"

"Yeah," I say. "He's good at that."

"And it makes you feel safe, right?"

"Well, I don't know," I tell her. What I don't say out loud is I don't think I'll ever feel safe again.

As if reading my thoughts, she says, "I don't know if I could ever feel safe again with anyone. I mean Marilyn's father was a doll when I met him. Who could have imagined he would turn into a total psycho?"

"Well, I don't think Jim would change like that," I say. "At least I hope not."

"Oh," she says, embarrassed again. "I didn't mean to imply that he would or could for that matter."

"I didn't think you did," I tell her.

"Do you love him?" she asks.

I turn towards her.

"It's probably none of my business," she says.

"No, it's okay," I say. "The truth is I don't know. I hadn't given it much thought. Besides he hasn't asked. Nor has he said he loves me, so it's been okay."

"Well, if he did," she asks. "If he did ask, how would you feel?"

And I don't know what to tell her, so I simply shrug and we both sit on our stools, watching it go from dusk to total darkness in what seems like seconds, with just the flickering lights from houses in the distance or a car on the road until the conductor announces that we're pulling into Stamford.

"Do you think you'll ever perform again?" she asks and then quickly catches herself: "Christ! Sorry, I don't know why I'm so filled with questions. I hate when people do that to me."

"I sort of like it," I say. "Jim doesn't ask much. He assumes that what he sees is all there is." I start to laugh.

"What's funny?" she asks.

"It's just that Don and I used to talk in lyrics and for some reason I've been thinking about that today and there I go doing it. You know, 'Is That All There Is?'"

"Peggy Lee," she says.

"Right. Anyway, forget it. It's silly."

"No, that sounds like fun. Truth is I always wanted to be a singer, just couldn't carry a tune. But I always learned the words. I'd stand in front of the mirror in my room, the music blasting and mouth the words of every song that came on the radio."

"'All or Nothing at All,'" I say.

And she answers, "'With a Song in My Heart!'" and the two of us burst out laughing and I go get us another wine.

"You really should sing again," she says. "Your face just lit up. I don't mean this like it sounds, but for a second there you looked ten years younger."

"You too," I say and we laugh again.

The conductor walks by. "You gals going to New York?"

"Philly/Baltimore," we say in unison. We're now giggling. He gives us a disapproving look, which only makes us giggle more.

"Well, there'll be a thirty-minute layover in New York," he says. "Then we close the bar."

"'Say It Isn't So,'" Irene chimes in.

And I say, "'Set 'em up, Joe,'" and the two of us are practically on the floor screeching with laughter.

"I haven't laughed like this in ages," I gasp trying to catch my breath.

"Me neither," she says.

We carry on like that the rest of the way to New York, coming up with lyrics, trying to make complete thoughts and sentences, having just a crazy time of it until one of us, or both, I'm not sure which, says, we should stay in touch and, I don't know why, but maybe because we know it'll never happen, we both sober up.

Then, she says–and it's definitely her who says it–"Maybe we should be getting back." "You're right," I say.

And as if she hasn't heard me she says, "I really should be checking on Marilyn."

"No, you're right," I repeat. "And I Jim."

And that's what we do. We walk back slowly, this time with Irene leading the way, again holding onto the backs of seats. When we get to our car, I can see Jim checking his e-mail on the Blackberry, holding it at an angle so the kid can watch. As we get close, Irene says something and the kid's face lights up, as does Jim's at seeing me. We rearrange ourselves. The kid back in front with Irene. Jim buried in his Blackberry. And me? Well, the truth is I'd love to be able to get off the train the minute we hit New York, and head straight up to the Algonquin.

Re-unions

Re-unions

I could have turned back. Said I changed my mind. He certainly gave me the option. But I've got this thing about going back on my word no matter what the consequences. So there I was with a total stranger, in a car—more like a small truck–on an unlit back road outside Asheville, wondering if I was going to live to tell the tale. All because I promised Betts I'd show her how to pick up a man for a one-night stand. But then, in those days, I was a teacher. Taught kids at a private school how to draw, paint, model clay, that sort of thing. (For the record, that thing about those who can do and those who can't teach? Well, it's crap. There's such a thing as putting food in your mouth.)

Anyway, back then private schools didn't require a teaching degree, so those of us who had dropped out of college, or decided not to go in the first place—I was one of the former–could usually get hired at one of them. It was also why they could get away with paying us next to nothing. In other words, I had no money, which is why– for three years in a row–I'd gone down to Betts over the Easter break instead of taking a real vacation, and why three years later I was driving to a stranger's house in the boonies for a night of unwanted sex.

Weird, the unwanted part. I mean, considering that year's dearth of partners and my heightened state of heat caused by aforesaid dearth, I should have been raring to go. But the moment I got in the car, not even a twitch. Seems like once Betts was no longer around to catch my how-to performance, going to bed with this man was more than anticlimactic–it was downright unnecessary. Let's be clear. It was not Betts fault. She was a good friend who had just gone through a miserable divorce, and was desperate. Well, who wouldn't be after living with a man who hadn't laid a loving hand on her for the last five of their sixteen years together?

Well, that's not entirely true. His hands were on her when others were around. Like the morning of my first visit three years earlier. She and I were in our robes—mine, one of her guest Terries and hers a very boudoir white silk with lace and just as she was about to pour us coffee, he entered– all suited up for the office, real pinstriped attorney style. He put down his brief case, wrapped his arms around her waist, picking her up so that her feet dangled–keeping his eyes on me the whole time. Then he squeezed until her back cracked and she let out an "Oh, Jim!" which could have meant anything from "Thanks, I needed that" to "Cut the crap!" It was hard to tell. By that time Betts had turned into the Barbie doll version of a Stepford wife. I couldn't believe him. I mean had he really thought he was fooling me? He'd made a pass just the night before.

It happened while we were having my welcome-to-the-South drinks at their bar. A really fabulous set-up you don't see often see in Manhattan apartments—all hickory with one of those tops that flip back so you can stand behind and play bartender. Anyway, Betts went to the kitchen to get us something to go with our drinks and suddenly there it was: a real grab ass hand on me. Of course I slapped it away, but that didn't wipe the "I know you want it" leer off his face. Wasn't the first time a friend's husband had pulled that stunt. Men see an unattached female and assume she's either a nympho who couldn't say no even if she wanted to, or gay and just needed the right man to turn her straight—I was neither.

I'd gone expecting a week of R and R. "Now Laura sweetie," Betts had said. "You really do need a break now, you hear?" Back in college she talked like the rest of us from New York, but once down South, she turned into Miss Scarlet herself, complete with drawl and lilt. "You've never tasted southern hospitality, now have you?" Years of living in Asheville had gotten to her. Either that or she'd felt she had to out-southern the southerners to be accepted.

It had been ages since we'd been in touch. Not like in the early years after they moved down to where Jim had roots. Back then she'd find every excuse to come up to New York. We'd go shopping—well, she shopped; I watched—meet for lunch and sometimes the three of us had dinner when he came with her. He was all over her then, refuting my Dad's, "If they make a big display in public, nothing's going on at home." And she did radiate satisfaction.

But after Jim, Jr. was born, our lives moved in vastly different directions—as did what we cared about. She: Jim, Jim Jr., who she met at the country club and what she served to whom when she entertained; me: how to make ends meet, the lack of time and energy to produce my own work, and the absence of a social life, i.e., a man. There came a point where our past no longer bound and the present split us apart. In the space of a few years we'd gone from college roommates who confided every thought we had, to phone calls on or around our birthdays, along with the obligatory Christmas cards. Mine were in whatever medium I was playing with that year: gouache; lithos; montage; Betts's a photographic chronicle—Hallmark style—of her existence: she and Jim cozied up in front of a fireplace; then the two of them in the nursery with Jim Jr.; followed by all of them posed with their dog in front of a house with two columns; then another dog and a newer house with more columns—along with an imprinted message. I did take note how rigid her smile had become, but figured, that unlike me, she was exhausted from holiday demands.

Then out of the blue came her call. ESP I told her. I wasn't lying; I had been thinking about her. "Decade-al accounting" I called it. My ten-year assessment of accomplishments, or lack thereof, as was the case with me.

"You've just got to come, Laura," she said. "Why we can celebrate reaching forty together. It'll be such fun." The fact that my birthday had passed, and hers was two months away, was overlooked.

At first I declined. The idea of visiting a one-time peer who now lived in the perfect house, had the perfect marriage, the perfect kid—not to mention those dogs—seemed way too masochistic even for me.

But in steel magnolia style she persisted and eventually the allure of mint juleps, or at least a better scotch than I could afford, along with plush comfortable chairs to sink into, warmer weather, and a few days off from having to fend for myself, won out. I set aside my qualms that envy might get the better of me and send me spiraling down deeper into the depression I was already heading towards, and said "You've got me–for better or worse."

On the flight down, I sat next to an attractive, ring-less man–somewhere around my age–with smiley eyes that spelled seduction. I can't remember which of us initiated the conversation, but once we started we didn't stop. We talked about politics, careers, what it was like to live in New York, what it was like to live in Asheville. I kept trying to figure out if there were a wife and kids in the picture, but he didn't allude to any, so I allowed my mind to race ahead full speed. Would he consider moving to New York if he and I went the whole nine yards? Could I live in the South? I was at the point of considering dual commuting when the plane landed.

We left the plane together–a smashing couple if I do say so. Anyway, there was Betts waving at me, and a woman whom I assumed to be a friend of hers–a real plain Jane–waving as well. I waved back. Then I realized he was waving too, but at the plain Jane. I managed to keep smiling. Wife-y did the same. We met up, introduced ourselves, and it took no more than a minute before Plain Jane whisked him away in one direction, and Betts and I went off in another. Interesting how gorgeous men choose their opposites, isn't it?

Betts and I were a study in contrasts: she in a spotless white, buttoned-down, ironed cotton blouse, a blue and green tartan plaid pleated skirt that came just above her knees, a blue matching cardigan, stockings and white sneakers. Me? Flowered cotton pants, flowery East Indian top, sandals and long dangly earrings.

Anyway, as we headed towards the car, Betts whispered, "I can't imagine how you managed that. Why you snagged the best looking man on board."

"Just got lucky with my seat, Betts. Not that it makes any difference. Obviously he's taken. Damn! I haven't had sex in over six months." And what did Betts say? The woman who I would have sworn was getting it regularly? The woman who had the marriage made in heaven?

"Lucky you–it's been almost five years for me!"

Well, I could have fallen down. I stopped to see if she was kidding, but she looked as if she could burst into tears.

"I can't tell you how relieved I am to have you here, Laura," she said. "Why I've had no one to speak with about any of this."

"What about all your friends from the Club?"

And, as if I should have known, she said, "They may be friends, but they're not confidantes. Anything I say could get back to Jim and that would be the end of me. Besides, the women down here stay away from even a hint of marital discord that could lead to divorce–afraid of giving their husbands any ideas."

So much for my free R&R. As my Dad used to say– he had a lot of sayings—"Everything has its price." Whatever small pangs of guilt I felt about only bringing a book of phantasmagoria for Jim, Jr. and two dozen New York bagels for Betts and me vanished. It was clear that my room and board had a price: My ears!

"You have no idea what it's like here, Laura. All the lawyers belong to the same club. I don't mean literally. Just that it's perfectly fine for them to fight each other down to the last golf ball for a client, as long as the client isn't one of their wives. Then it's as if they're all at the same firm. Between Jim and his connections, I could lose everything, including Jim, Jr."

Listening to Betts go on about the facade of her marriage, the lack of any real communication amongst friends, the charade she'd carried on, I wasn't sure how I'd last the week. When we arrived at the house, I really panicked. It was "House Beautiful" southern style. The silver displayed and polished, chotzkes all over the place without a speck of dust, and her needlepoint pillows on every chair and sofa. I began to imagine Betts mentally jabbing Jim, Sr. with every stitch. It was obvious we now lived in two completely different worlds. I relished my alone time; Betts needed to talk. While she'd been living in a '50's movie, I'd marched against the war, smoked pot, picked up men at bars, and went to meetings about women's sexuality where we stared at our vulvas and taught ourselves the art of the dildo. How we were going to find common ground eluded me.

Thankfully, Jim., Sr. decided to take Jim, Jr., camping and slowly the old Betts began to emerge. Not all of her, but enough so she was recognizable in spite of her white sneakers that stayed white. Now, don't get me wrong, it wasn't all one-sided. Betts did ask questions about my life. Especially the sexual part. Seems while I was racking up more men than I could count, Jim had been it for her. Were we envious of each other? Not sure. I certainly couldn't have turned myself inside out for as long as she had to keep a man around, and I'm sure she couldn't imagine being in bed with someone to whom she wasn't committed. Still, by the end of my visit, she decided she'd had enough as far as Jim was concerned. The fact he made a pass at me–I told her what had happened once he left the premises–was probably the proverbial straw.

It took a few months, but eventually she found a lawyer up in Raleigh. A female. One who'd been so screwed by her first husband that she'd returned to school and gotten her law degree just so she could reap revenge by proxy. If her clients' husbands were lawyers, as hers had been, so much the better. As the news got out, Betts began to hear stories about Jim's groping hands; the women he'd pawed right out in the open; the secretary he'd been screwing forever. I never asked her what it was like to have spent years creating the perfect home only to find out that everyone knew it a lie. Just knew the shame had to be enormous.

By the time I returned the following Easter, Betts and Jim were still battling over the fine print. Betts's lawyer hadn't let her move out, and Jim knew enough to stay as well so as not to lose his claim on the property. I pitied their kid. He had to negotiate his way between the two of them on a daily basis. Not that I ever saw the younger Jim more than one night a year, the Easter camping trip now a ritual. Still, it only took a quick glance at his drawn face and wary eyes, to know some shrink was going to have a field day down the road.

Finally, around February of the next year, before my third visit, a settlement was reached. Jim Sr. would officially move out so there would be no break in Jim Jr.'s living arrangements. After seven years, when Jim Jr. was ready for college, Betts would be expected to be self-supporting. Jim Sr., would buy her share of the house-not that he wanted to live there; he just didn't want her to. By March his clothes were gone, along with some of the furniture, and he rented a place within walking distance for Jim Jr. Then, in April, I arrived with two bottles of champagne—one for each of us.

The first night, after Betts bundled Jim Jr. off to Jim Sr.'s, she and I got into our robes—warm flannel affairs-curled up in her cushioned chairs in the den, and cracked open the first bottle. Catch-up wasn't needed. By now we were on the phone at least once a week. I was getting pleasantly soused when I became aware of a car slowly driving back and forth in front of the house. I looked quizzically at Betts. "It's Jim," she said. "He drives by every night to remind me I'm a boarder and better not damage his property." I asked what she was going to do, not about Jim, but in general. "Don't know. The only job I had was at that publishing house, remember? Was more a flunky than anything else. I could go back to school and get a Masters in something. Jim would have to pay-my lawyer made sure to put that in our agreement. I don't know, Laura. I'm still trying to figure it out."

All celebrating had ended with my question. The Stepford wife was gone, but at what price? She sounded beaten. I started to get "the guilts." Not that I had talked her into leaving Jim. If she hadn't wanted to, she'd never have invited me in the first place. Of all the people in her life, she knew I'd be the one to urge her to go it alone. Still, somehow I felt the need to make it better. So, if I couldn't help her out with career advice-hell, I was having enough trouble with my own-at least I could demonstrate how to get laid.

"Listen," I said. "How about we get out of here tomorrow night? Go to a bar or something. We might even meet some men. You never know."

"Oh, I don't know." she said.

"Why not? The divorce is final. You're on your own. You might even find someone to bed. You never can tell."

"I wouldn't know how."

"For Christ's sake. It's like riding a bike."

"I didn't mean how to have sex. Just how to pick someone up."

"So, I'll show you." And with a bit more coaxing that was it. We spent the next hour figuring out which restaurant in the area had a bar that catered to singles. We decided on two places and the next day drove by to see which one looked more appealing. They appeared identical, with their painted white fronts, blue awnings, parking lots in the rear. I couldn't tell the difference; however, Betts could.

"This one would get a better crowd," she said.

How she knew that, beat me. "Whichever makes you comfortable," I told her.

We spent the rest of the day dolling ourselves up. I even put on makeup. Then, at seven thirty sharp, we went off in search of prey.

I quickly realized I was in alien territory. In New York, I could tell what someone did by the bar they chose. The White Horse got mostly writers and actors. Fanelli's the artists, especially those who had to teach to supplement their incomes. The Cedar Tavern mostly tourists and art students who thought they could improve their output by rubbing up against the walls where Pollack once stood. Max's Kansas City got the more swinging crowd of photographers, models and the current hot art world names. Even if you hit a night where no one went where they were expected to go, you still could get a feel as to who was who by their appearance. The painters always had some paint splattered on them somewhere; the sculptors proudly displayed their cuts, bruises and burn marks of the day, and the photographers, lived in black pants, black shirts, black shoes and either shaved their heads or sported ponytails. In those days, the male artists outnumbered us females twenty to one. Still I had to compete against art students or would-be artist's wives for a man's attention. And sure, I could mistake a fragile looking conceptual artist–the kind who built landscapes out of sand and sticks—for a writer, but by and large I knew who was who. (There was the night of the plumber, but he'd hung around the art scene for so long, who could tell?) Anyway, in Asheville, I was totally out of my element. These guys could have worked for the phone company stringing lines, bagging groceries or worked for the electric company. With no markers to go by, I imagined them all spending their weekends shooting guns, racing cars or roping cattle, although I was perfectly aware we were way too far east for that.

We'd been sitting at the bar for about fifteen minutes when I noticed this guy perched on a stool down at the far end. It was hard to tell his height, but he looked relatively cute, light brown hair, good build. I told Betts to watch and smiled at him. Not a full smile–just a subtle tease. He nodded back with an imperceptible movement of the head. I turned back to Betts.

"That's the opener."

"Really? That's it?"

"That's it. Act One Scene One."

"How do you get it from that to, well, you know?"

So I tilt my head towards him again and then back towards us, suggesting he come over. Which, of course, he does. So far, not so different from New York. Can't tell what he does for a living from his khaki pants and white polo shirt. Just before he slides into the stool next to me, I whisper to Beth, "In for a penny. . ."

From there it was easy. A little conversation, followed by a foot, mine, resting on his shoe. I figured I would tell Betts about the foot thing later. After a while Betts got the message that he and I were into each other. Which, for the moment, I was. So she excused herself. Said she's tired. "Now you stay as long as you want, Laura, you hear? And you, sir, you bring her home safe and sound." The southern belle was back.

That was it. For the first half of the ride, we didn't say much of anything. Then I confessed. Told him that it had all been a show for my friend. That's when he asked if I wanted to turn back, and even though I wanted to say yes, I couldn't bring myself to do so. Sort of like that old joke about losing your virginity because you didn't want to appear rude. Besides, part of me was curious. Not about him. But about whether I would make it out alive. I'm serious. My life had been so drab of late that the thought of tempting fate appealed. Ten years of teaching kids that could care less. Rejection after rejection at galleries. The longest relationship I'd managed to sustain was probably just over two weeks, the exceptions being one or two European artists who I'd see when they came to town. Meanwhile most of my friends seemed to be moving on with their lives. Even Betts had made a change. It's not that I wanted to get killed or anything like that. Nor was I making some crazy pact with God. You know, Oh Lord, get me out of this alive and I promise to change my ways. Nothing like that. Maybe I thought that by courting danger I could shake things up a bit.

Eventually we arrived at what appeared to be a one-level shack plopped down in the middle of a wooded area—the southern kind. Less lush than we have up north. Trees that looked like they were a cross between a huge oak and a palm. Not that I could see much. It was pitch black. He left the car lights on and got out. Didn't come around to my side and open the car door or anything. Just got out and expected I'd follow. I imagined I'd find a bed, cans of beer on the floor, and a lantern. Where the lantern idea came from, I'm not sure except that I figured no one bothered to string electrical wires this far out. He walked onto the porch, unlocked the door, flicked on an actual light switch, and stood there waiting for me to enter. Well you wouldn't have believed it. I certainly didn't. There along the wall, the one to my left, hung three Mondrians, one Matisse, and a Kline. Not originals, obviously. Prints. How the hell did he know from Kline?

"Not bad for a redneck, huh?" he said.

And I didn't know what to say. "You've got great taste," was all I could come up with. He must have been waiting for this moment the whole ride out.

I forced my eyes away from the wall and looked around. The place was similar to mine, only smaller. One open room with a fridge, stove, and counter along the wall to the right. A round table in the middle. A few chairs. Small sofa. A bed, double. And then, lining the back wall, windows. His furniture wasn't half bad either. Leather, black, with some red pillows. Could have come right out of a magazine. It crossed my mind that maybe some woman had done it up for him or that he'd been married and this was what his ex no longer wanted. He became someone to find out about, but he wasn't interested in conversation. Took a beer, offered me one, which I refused, and headed towards the bed.

"It's late," he says.

"Right," I answer.

"We don't have to have sex," he says as we're on the bed slowly pulling off our clothes.

In retrospect, he probably felt as uninterested as I was. But back to my not reneging on an offer, I said, "No, it's okay." So he started in and I followed–like two bad dancers going through the motions. The sex was what was to be expected, lousy, though he did achieve orgasm. And no, I didn't fake one. Not that he cared. When he was done, he just rolled over after giving me one of those "there, there" pats on my rear. In New York I'd have gotten up and gone home. Here I had no choice. In for a penny, my eye.

When we got up, it was as if I didn't exist. He grabbed a beer out of the fridge, and when I said "good morning," he demanded that I get a move on so he wouldn't be late for work. I can't remember what kind of work he did, or if he even told me. Most likely he did, but it was so removed from my world that it never registered. We drove to Betts's in silence. I kept trying to figure out what I'd say to her. If I was honest how lousy a night I'd had, she might not ever try it for herself, and that would be a real waste of my energies. I was fantasizing a long shower when he pulled up to the curb, reached across me to open my door, and made a big thing of time passing by drumming his fingers on the wheel. I think I made some dumb remark like, "Well, you know where we are," as I got out, and walked up the driveway fully expecting to see Betts rushing out to greet me. Instead there was a note pinned on the front door: L, I'm at Charlotte Memorial, Jim Jr. hurt. Meet me there. B

I'm sure Betts figured that my so-called date would drive me to the hospital, but he was long gone so I had to run to a neighbor's house. The wife called me a cab, and off I went. I can tell you that for the next few days, until it was clear that Jim Jr. was going to be fine— he'd fallen into a ravine and hit his head—the last thing on either of our minds was what kind of night I'd had. By the time it did come up all I told her about was the art work on the redneck's walls. It sufficed.

A few months later Betts called all excited. Friends had arranged for her to meet a man they knew, a business associate. "A blind date, Laura. Can you imagine? Supposedly, he's dated everyone between here and Charlotte. Oh, Laura, I'm a nervous wreck. It's been years since I've been with someone other than Jim. I feel like a school girl."

I told her she'd do just fine and called the next day to see how it went.

"Fine," her answer.

"There's got to be more than just 'fine.'"

And she said, "Well, he's divorced. A realtor. Two kids. They live with the mother." "

"Is he cute at least?"

"Nice looking," she answered, in a rather matter-of-fact way, which told me there was no attraction.

"If there's one, there's two," I said.

"Maybe, I'm not sure."

"Well, I am."

"Slim pickings around here," her response.

She went out with him again. And again. And then again.

"So, it's serious?"

"He's really nice, Laura. Very considerate. And there's not a lawyer in his family," the southern accent returning. Only this go-round it has less of an edge.

I asked what she's doing about finding work, and she said she'd talked with various people, but no one had any ideas. "One even told me to get a job as a saleswoman. I mean, really! Now, I'm not denigrating sales people, Laura, but a sales woman's job is not going to support me, not one tiny bit."

So I said, "Maybe you could go work for a decorator. Or open a needlepoint store. You certainly know how to do both of those."

"A thought," she said, but there was no excitement in her voice.

Betts and I talked less and less as she and Marlin—that was his name, Marlin—continued to see each other. It was obvious he was staying overnight the weekends Jim Jr. was with his dad. Not that she came right out and told me. I asked her once how the sex was and all I got back was an, "Oh, Laura." It sounded no different from her old "Oh, Jim." She did invite me to come down the next year, but it didn't seem right to go, her being in a new relationship and all. She didn't sound disappointed either when I said I couldn't. I also didn't make it to the wedding. Can't remember why exactly. Probably too much money for an overnighter what with air fare, hotel, cabs and everything. For a time we went back to the phone calls around our birthdays and the ever present Christmas cards, both of ours now bought at card shops. Then the calls stopped, and a few years ago, so did the cards. I can only assume she's okay with her life. I'm sure happier with mine. Finally landed a decent gallery. Had a one-woman show. Even sold some paintings! Now I'm getting ready for the next. Every so often I wonder whose wall my work will end up on. I mean you never know, do you?

Stopping Time

Stopping Time

Wednesday, September 17, 3:05p.m.

A part of my brain is frozen. Another part has this weird idea that the doctor's pronouncement is my just desserts for hating suspense. That this entire scenario is tied to my life-long habit of skipping to the last page. That's it, isn't it? Due to my refusal to read along, moment by moment, page by page, without knowing how a story ends, I have been sentenced to death–the time and date approximate, but definite to occur. Well, I promise never to skip ahead again, doctor. Will that change anything?

"Mrs. Sopher, did you understand what I just said? Without treatment you have approximately four, six months at the outside."

"It's Ms." Am I crazy? Standing on ceremony? Now?

"Ms. Sopher. Did you hear me?"

"What?"

"I'm trying to explain. Without treatment you could have approximately no more than six months."

"And with?" I say. At least I think it's me. No one else appears to be in the room except the doctor–and his mouth is closed.

"We should be able to extend your life a bit," the suspense-ender says.

"What's a bit?"

"Perhaps to eight. Maybe more. One never knows exactly."

"Is that including or in addition to the original four to six?" I sound like a math teacher and I flunked math. A math-flunker has just entered into a discussion with a suspense-ender as to whether six to eight equals two to four or eight to twelve.

"Including."

"And how much of the time will I be able to work?" My question is more than valid. I have seen the ravages of chemotherapy and radiation. Watched friends go through hell in the hope of one more day. For naught, as they say.

The doc seems edgy. My inquisitiveness has put him off. It's a shame doctors don't appreciate patients with inquiring minds. Curiosity produced the tools of their trade. Without it there would be no penicillin, no aspirin, no sutures, no heart transplants, no lung–

He's saying something. I try to tune in.

". . . You could have some bad days. Perhaps a week out of each month."

"Which would bring me back to the original four to six of productivity, correct?" I am greatly impressed with my newfound mathematical prowess. It is incredible how learning you have inoperable lung cancer improves the mathematical quadrant of your brain–even more than listening to Mozart. I would so love to be listening to Mozart.

"You could look at it that way," he says.

"Look at what, what way?"

"Some time may be lost to treatment."

I can't believe I'm here listening to a doctor, who I've seen only once before, inform me I will not live to see my sixty-second birthday, my daughter's thirty-fifth year, my granddaughter's second, or my lover's paunch as it changes shape. I want to be pressed to Roger's paunch. I must make certain he doesn't go on a diet. I need to fold into whatever extra weight he has. Sink into his body and hold on.

"If I choose to do nothing, then what?" A dumb question. I'm hardly breathing as it is.

"You'll get progressively worse."

I wonder how that's possible. What's worse than not being able to breathe without awareness as one walks across a room, or lies in bed, or attempts to down a glass of scotch? Gasping for air certainly is a bummer. Shit! I am going to be deprived of a Hollywood ending.

126

No walk on a beach with music playing in the background. No wind blowing through my hair with dog at my side. No staring out at the water imagining my ashes transported away. I'm not sure about the ashes. All that fire and smoke. I could ask to be placed on a barge or an ice floe. It's what Eskimos do. Step out onto the ice and drift away. As long as there are no sharks. I do not relish being eaten–alive or dead. Then again, I don't want to be shoveled into the ground. Too damn claustrophobic.

On the other hand, I could will my body to a medical school, except I've heard med students stand around and crack awful jokes about their cadavers. Not for me. I've worked too bloody hard to maintain my image. Fought to be taken seriously. It's been years since I donned a bathing suit for fear of producing a smirk. Of course, Roger has seen me naked, but he loves me enough to leave his glasses on the night stand as we hit the sack. I could make it a prerequisite: I will leave my body to medicine as long as you treat it with great respect. And you must give my eyes to someone worthy. A blind artist. Or a photographer losing his or her sight. As long as the work is of a high caliber. I'll be damned if my eyes will spend someone else's lifetime looking at cute babies or Martha Stewart flower arrangements.

"Do you have any questions?" the doctor asks.

Yes. Yes, I do. Like didn't your mother teach you any manners? Didn't she tell you it's impolite to tell someone something they can do nothing about? One time, at the Post Office, a stranger stopped to tell me I had a run in my stocking. On my way to a job interview yet! Of course she couldn't have known where I was going, but if she didn't have a pair of pantyhose in my size and color ready and waiting, along with a discreet place for changing, then she had no business opening her mouth. You have no manners young man. And you are so damn young! Oh God, I envy the time you have.

"Do you have any questions, Mrs., Ms. Sopher?"

I don't think so. I'm not even certain if I'm still attached to my body.

"Is there someone you would like me to call to take you home?"

I can't imagine why he thinks I should need anyone. I'm not any sicker now than when I walked in. Anyway, what's the worst that could happen? I leave the building, step off the curb in front of a moving car, and I'm instantly gone. My HMO would save a fortune in hospice care and morphine drips. As for the driver, once he realizes he and his car performed an act of kindness, he'll get over the guilts.

"Please, you shouldn't be alone."

"I think better alone," I say, although I'm not sure what I'm supposed to put my mind to. We're taught to think about what we're to do with our life; trained to set daily, weekly, monthly goals that extend well into our future; we're not accustomed to think in finite terms.

It's obvious he expects me to get up. To vacate the office so he can move on to his next victim. But my legs won't move. Nor do I wish to find a way to make them. If I don't move, time will stop, and the countdown can't begin.

"Well, then, if you have no more questions. . ." He closes my file and buzzes for a nurse.

I have a question. How could this happen to me? It makes no sense. Not to me at least. I, who have survived the so-called Art World, a lousy ten year marriage, the deaths of friends, betrayals by so-called lovers, and still never took to my bed depressed. Except once. Once, I woke up, opened my eyes, saw a smudge on the wall and thought about my terrible ineptitude as a housekeeper. How by not keeping my walls smudge-free, I had provoked John to seduce student after student, and my marriage would not have disintegrated, and I would not be spiraling downwards into what even I could see was depressive thinking. I jumped out of bed and never permitted myself to think that way again. Now does a woman with that kind of strength, that ability to plow through life taking whatever it serves up, deserve this?

"I never smoked."

"Many lung cancer patients never did. We just don't know the reasons yet."

Suddenly he's a 'we.' Faced with a question he cannot answer, he no longer takes individual responsibility.

I will not get out of this chair. I will not let time move forward. I will place my hands underneath the seat and hold on for dear life. He and his nurse will have to carry me out, chair and all. They did that at my wedding. Placed me on a chair, lifted me up, and danced me around, my gown floating over their heads. They lifted John in his chair as well. Carried us both aloft, our hands stretched out to each other as they swayed us to the music. Long live the king and queen! May they have a happy future! A lot of good that did.

"Why don't you let my nurse call someone?"

He has omitted using my name. So besides being a suspense-ender, he's a play-it-safer as well. He checks his notes.

"You have a daughter, don't you? Perhaps we could call her."

"She's on vacation."

I stay seated. I know it's impolite to overstay one's welcome, and I don't mean to be rude. I have always followed Miss Manners to the letter. Before her, I read Emily Post. Both teach courtesy. And I always try to extend it, even to doctors. But now a doctor, this doctor, has told me I have approximately four months to live and as Judith Martin, to my knowledge, has not yet addressed how to behave in this situation, I have no rules to follow. So, I will stay, uninvited, rudely occupying space in this doctor's office, for as long as we both shall live.

3:17p.m. I am being moved by two guards dressed as nurses, through a strangely out-of-focus room filled with people, down the hole of the elevator, out onto the sidewalk where the world has obviously gone mad. People walk along as if nothing has changed. Horns honk. Cars move. My life is about to stop and no one is acknowledging it. People, say something! But the only ones who talk are the two white garbed figures firmly fixed to my sides with their constant barrage of "Are you all right, Mrs. Sopher?" "Isn't there someone we could call?" You shouldn't be alone right now." One of them hollers, "Taxi!" waving anxiously as if I were late for an appointment. As if a cab will come and whisk me away. This is New York, you idiot.

They make it obvious they want me to disappear. I could go for that. There is nothing I would like more right now than to walk away, leave my body behind, and keep going until no one, including myself, can find me.

"Taxi!" she hollers even louder. And wouldn't you know, one actually pulls up? Aha! That's why they sent her down with me. She knows how to move time forward. A cool cookie my father would have called her. She opens the door and they both usher me in. "Good-bye, Mrs. Sopher," they say in unison. Are they so afraid I'll take them with me? I heard that somewhere. Beware of the dying. They don't want to go alone. Well, don't worry, you two, I don't want to go with me either.

3:25p.m. "Where to, Lady?" the driver asks.

I haven't the vaguest idea. Where does someone go who is about to die?

"Lady?"

"I don't know."

"You must go somewhere. I turn this cab into garage in half hour." He can't be more than thirty. Afghani, Indian, Turkish? The specific ethnicity of this new onslaught of drivers escapes me.

I look in my purse. I've got thirty dollars and some change. "How far will thirty-two dollars take me?" My mathematical abilities seem to be diminishing rapidly.

"My garage is near LaGuardia. You want to go there?"

Why not? I could get on a plane, although with my luck the only one available will land in Pittsburgh. I have a sudden urge to go to the beach. To walk along the sand into the ocean. "Can you drive me to a beach? We could stop at an ATM. I could get whatever you want." Money, obviously, no longer an issue.

"Lady, you want beach? I take you to ATM. You get out. Find another cab."

"Just start driving. I'll figure it out."

He throws the meter and edges forward into the traffic. For a brief period they had recordings in cabs telling you to buckle up. As if any real New Yorker would. It's the daily risk that keeps one alive here. That's it! He can drive me to the Major Deegan and let me out in the middle of the road. If I survive, then I'm not meant to die after all. Oh, God! I'm going to die.

"Lady, you better decide soon or I have to let you out."

"Where would you go if you were going to die?" I ask.

"What?"

I repeat my question, the light turns red, the cab lurches to a stop and he turns around. His eyes are fierce. Beautiful. Thirty years ago I would have bedded him in a flash.

"You going to die?"

I nod, slowly. My body is imperceptibly rocking back and forth as if I were dovening. I will not pray. You don't turn to God just because you've been given a death sentence.

"Lady, you really going to die?" he repeats.

I nod. "In four months. Four months." Repeating it doesn't make it any more real.

"I'm sorry, Lady."

It's not what I want him to say. I want him to tell me it's not true, that I'm too young to die. Why doesn't he get into the back seat with me? Take me into his arms and tell me everything will be all right.

"I'm sorry," he repeats.

"So am I."

"You got someone at home?"

"Not at home exactly, but close enough."

"Then I take you there."

There's no stopping this ride, is there?

5:10p.m. This hand that's clicked a shutter high overhead and gotten clear, perfect shots, cannot steady itself to dial a goddamn phone. Why the hell won't Roger's number come out of my fingers? A few hours ago I could have punched it in my sleep. I try again, slowly. Finally, I manage to hit all the right keys in the correct order. He picks up on the first ring.

"It's me," I say.

"Where are you?" His voice a tightrope.

"Here. Home." I don't mention I've been crunched up in this chair, my head buried in Mischa's fur, listening to Roger's messages for almost two hours. I know he's opening and closing his hand. His way of keeping his fingers from stiffening. His way of easing tension. Mine are still shaking. Silence.

"Roger?"

"What did he say?" His voice is taut, brittle, controlled.

My resolve to pretend all is well, pick a fight then send him away in one grand gesture crumbles. "Not good." I say.

"How not good?"

"Bad. As a matter of fact, extremely bad." I shouldn't be flip, but I can't help it. I must keep it all at a distance. "Listen," I say, before he can find words. "You don't have to run over. I'm okay."

"Have you called Kate?" He says.

"Of course not." You call your daughter when you've got it together. When you know you won't splinter. When you're certain the glue will hold. "I'm not having her cut her vacation short."

"I'm coming over." He doesn't sound as if he wants to move from where he is either. Who can blame him?

"You don't have to. I've got Mischa." Brilliant! Tell your lover he's been replaced by your dog. "I mean he needs to be walked." I want things back to normal: Come when you want. If you want. Whenever. The way we have played it for the past two years.

"I'll walk him when I get there."

"I can do it."

"Soph, I'll do it when I get there!" He's angry. "Mischa can wait for Christ's sake."

"Then I'll get into the shower." Showers help me start a day over. There have been days when I've showered two, three, four times. I am drenched in guilt. Roger can't lose another woman.

5:40p.m. It's surreal. I am standing in a closet, wrapped in a towel, trying to decide what to wear. Is that what a sane person does? Is this what Mary Queen of Scots did? Worry about what she should wear after she was condemned to death? Or Marie Antoinette? Ethel Rosenberg had it easy. Prison garb. I wonder if they allowed her lipstick. I should put some on. I probably look like Morticia Addams. Christ! Look at it all: black, black, and more black. Talk about being prepared for a funeral.

"Soph?"

So soon?

"In in here." The voice that could command a Goliath to sit, turn, get out of the way, cannot carry past the closet door. I take in whatever breath I can and try again. "Here!"

Roger is carrying Mischa's leash. I can usually read my subject, but this one has shielded himself from any penetration. It's as if there's a concrete boulder between us. He stands stone-like in the doorway while Mischa paws at him begging to go out. "What exactly did he say?" he asks.

"Four to six months." He doesn't need more explanation; he's been here before.

"What about treatment?"

"Ah, to treat or not to treat . . . it's not a question."

"Did he say that or did you?"

"Treatment offered. Rejected."

"Not good enough, Soph. Exactly what did he say?"

His voice hasn't lost its resonance. It was his voice that attracted even before I saw the body it inhabited. "Why only black and white?" he asked. And because he sounded as if he really wanted to know, I turned and answered, "Because of all the greys."

"Soph! What did he say?"

"It could buy me a few months. Not worth it." I want him to tell me none of this is real. That treatment will work. He doesn't.

"We'll get a second opinion, Soph. Doctors make mistakes."

"A waste of time."

"Another opinion!"

"I can put the time to better use."

"Really? Like what?" Sarcasm doesn't become him, but I don't tell him that.

"Like archiving the last ten years of my work. Zander has been after me to do it. If not now, when?"

"I want another opinion."

"Well, maybe I don't!" And before I can stop myself out comes, "I don't think you should hang around. I mean it. Go! Escape while you can."

"And where would you have me go?" His voice now a string pulled tight.

"Don't tell me you want to go through this again."

And he explodes. "Of course I don't want to go through this again. I don't want to see you go through this either. But I'm not cutting out. Who the hell do you think you've been with these last two years?"

"I just don't want you staying because you think it's the right thing to do."

"Well, too bad, Soph, because it is the right thing to do. It's also the only thing I can do. So, don't pick a fight with me, Soph. I know the routine. It won't work." He is back in control.

Anyway, I can't pull it off. I sink to the floor. He's right on top of me.

"I'm no Beth, Roger. I can't kill myself. I can't do it."

We're wrapped around each other. I can't tell whose sobs I'm feeling. His or mine. Naturally Mischa begins to pee.

Thursday September 18, 3:45a.m.

"Soph! What the hell are you doing? It's the middle of the night."

"Purging! No one but me gets to decides what will be shown. No one!" I continue to expose roll after roll of film. Tear up print after print. I need to control something.

"You'll regret this, Soph. Cut it out."

"There'll be no time for regrets."

"Stop damnit! Those are of Vieques. I want those. There as much mine as yours."

"I took them, they're mine. If I want to destroy them, I can."

"Not in your present state, you can't. Listen to me, Soph, you're not dying tomorrow. You've got time to sort through it all."

"No I don't! Don't you see, I don't!"

"Come back to bed, Soph. I need you there."

Friday September 26, 11:45a.m.

A morning spent with a lawyer on a will is bad enough when you think you're going to live. When you know you're not...

"I want to go to the beach."

"What?"

"I want to go to the beach."

"Soph, it's almost noon on a Friday. We wouldn't arrive until three, four o'clock."

"I don't care."

"What do you plan to do when we get there?"

"I don't know. Look out at the water. Build a sand castle. Take pictures."

He nods, sags, and goes to call the garage. Only days ago he'd have jumped at the idea, thrilled with his late-in-life acquired spontaneity. It's his lack of energy that confirms the new reality.

5:15p.m. "Go with Roger!" I order. Mischa has donned his dejected look. It used to make me laugh. Now it's painful to watch. He's so anxious. May he not be one of those dogs who senses his mistress's impending departure and dies of a broken heart. He's got years left to play. To be loved. Kate will love him. She has from the day he arrived.

"Sure you're warm enough?"

"Sure," although I don't think I'll ever be warm again.

They are quite a pair: a black overgrown terrier and a tall, slightly bowlegged, balding, sixty-seven year old man, with a slight paunch.

"We won't be long."

"No rush." We both need time alone. "Go with Roger!" I say again. Mischa cocks his head to confirm my permission and races to do battle with the tide as if each oncoming wave was there solely for his pleasure.

What a sight I must look, huddled in a blanket, oxygen tank attached, propped behind a tripod dug deep into the sand, camera perched on top. I focus my lens on the jutting rocks–remnants from another time. The gulls dive for fish and a few scavenge the beach. How I raged against the idiots who strew litter when John and I lived here. Campaigned to get it removed, pushing petitions into the hands of everyone I could corner. Now my eyes gloss over the debris and rest only on nature's doings. A tiny crab, desperate for shelter, burrows into the sand next to my foot. I wonder how long he'll live. Strange I never inquired before. Or, maybe I did and just can't remember. The beach is almost empty. A hooded couple walk along, their pants rolled up above their calves, wading through the water, oblivious to everything but each other. It's grey and bleak and beautiful.

An older woman, a brisk walker probably out for her evening constitution, calls, "Do you need anything?"

"No. Thanks," I say, but the wind blows what voice I have back at me causing my body to shudder. I, who have always luxuriated in aloneness, now experience small waves of anxiety when left by myself. It is such a new feeling. I reassure myself I'll more than survive until Roger gets back, and wave her on. Still she comes closer. Her short cropped hair exposed under her hood. Her weathered skin not yet visible from here, but reasonably imagined as her knobby knees poke through her grey sweats. She is what I should have become.

"Are you sure you're all right?" she asks.

There's no answer anyone would want to hear. I want to tell her this person she sees is not the real me. Not who I am. Not who I was. Maybe she thinks I'm in the early stages of emphysema with years left. But all I say is, "My friend's on a walk. I'm okay."

"Well, if you're sure." Her eyes penetrate quizzically.

"Do you know how long crabs live?" I ask between breaths as she turns to go.

"Never thought about it much. Lobsters can go for 20 years. I doubt if crabs can go that long. Probably a year or two if it survives us and the elements. Photographing crabs?"

I shake my head, no.

"Hard to talk?"

A smile and a nod.

"Well, I'll leave you alone then."

She moves off. I watch her go through the camera's lens and quell my desire to call her back. Such vanity on my part. Did I really expect to shoot a final series? Rita Sopher: On a beach in Amagansett, October 3, 2004. Zander will be disappointed. Posthumous shows always sell out. It would have been the perfect finale. The sea splashing up against the rocks. Spray rising high like an enormous fan. The conclusion of my "Water Series" started how many years ago? Thirty? Forty? Thirty-four. On our honeymoon. My only way to study John without self-consciousness getting in the way. And, he did like to be studied. No wonder I switched to rocks emerging from the sea, stone formations with jutting arches, worn away, yet still combative.

I have always wondered why people insist on taking pictures of themselves on vacations. As if looking at a shot of someone on top of a camel, or in front of a lopped-off Louvre, can give a sense of being there. The pungent smell of the dung. The sensual after-taste of an espresso. The whiff of a Galois. I lied to the doctor. I smoked. Not often. But enough.

If I had a shred of decency, I'd disconnect my oxygen right here and now and burrow down under the sand next to the crab. By the time Roger returned, we'd all be spared the next few months, and he wouldn't have to watch me waste away, until my eyes pop out from my skull, bones protrude through the skin, and my hair—what hair there'll be—comes out from my scalp in clumps. Wrong! Hair only falls away with chemo. Fantastic. I'll die with a full head of hair. Maybe I can get the nurses to enshroud me in a beautiful fabric. A thick silk filled with extraordinary colors and designs—gold, green, blue, with an incredibly long fringe—just like the one that hung over my mother's piano where I used to hide, waiting to see how long it would take an adult to realize I'd gone missing. No, the contrast would only make the image more grotesque. I am already losing color. I must tell Roger to warn Kate of what awaits her before she bursts in filled with joy. Oh, God, I dread seeing her see me.

"Soph?" Roger's voice and Mischa's tongue come at me all at once.

"You just left," I say.

"We've walked for a good hour, Soph. Here, got us some coffee."

I don't want coffee. I want the hour back. "I'm not ready to leave, Roger," I snap like a turtle. "I have pictures to take."

"I'm not stopping you, Soph."

I can't imagine he will risk another relationship. Two tortuous endings in a little less than five years are enough for anyone. Still, three's a charm. Maybe he'll go for a thirty-something who will promise to love and obey until death, knowing she'll have more than enough time to repeat the process. And here I agonized over starting up with him. Afraid I'd get attached and he'd be snatched from me. Shit. We're still young. We're supposed to have at least ten to twenty years together.

I wish I had Beth's guts. Be able to hoard pill after pill in one sacrosanct drawer of her night table so she could off herself before the time came. I too, might off myself if I had a year's warning. But four months, nine days of which I've already used up, is simply too short a time.

"Soph. I wish you'd call Kate. Have her come home sooner."

Why does he keep harping on this? Does he want to pawn me off on her?

"Back in a few days. Unless you know something, I don't. Like I'm about to expire."

"You're not about to expire, but she needs to be here."

"Trust me. She'll be grateful for every day she's spared."

What a miserable year she's in for. Mothers are supposed to hang around well into a child's fifties. At least I should. I'm young. Isn't sixty the new forty? Mom made it to eighty-one, Dad two more. Statistically I am supposed to live even longer. Well, at least Kate won't be saddled with having to take care of me in my declining years. No gut-wrenching decisions about whether I should move in with her and David, or be shipped off to a nursing home. And she once accused me of not being capable of positive thinking. Well, Katie Sopher Judson, you should hear me now.

"Damn!!" My wave crashes, its spume spreading over the rocks before my fingers can hit the shutter.

Roger moves and sits behind me, enveloping me in his legs. He places his hands over mine and waits. "There'll be another," he says.

"I love you," I rasp.

"Because I hold a mean camera?"

The wave will come. We'll get it. I'll give the best shot to Kate. She can keep it on her desk. Or put it in a drawer to be taken out on those nights when she feels a sudden need for her mother.

Monday, October 20, 11:30a.m.

"I'll get it, Mom," Katie yells. Between her and Roger, I no longer need to answer the phone. No loss. It was never my preferred means of communication. How long has Kate craved me to stay still only now to be the one running around busying herself with meaningless tasks? Be careful what you wish for, my darling.

Yesterday we tried a walk. We passed a new cosmetic store filled with counters where you can try on the latest colors. Painted our faces. Played as we never had. Is this what we missed? This morning I sit by a window. To do more would be an expenditure of energy I don't have.

The neighborhood has changed. Where have all the artists gone, long time passing . . . I have lived here twenty-nine years. We were pioneers, Katie and I. The area so desolate friends asked me to walk them to a cab, as if my five-foot six-inch frame could have protected them. My daughter returns.

"Mom, it's Dee. She wants to come by."

I don't want to see Dee. I don't want to see anyone. Or is it I don't want anyone to see me?

"M-o-m." Her voice hangs onto the middle vowel. It's the same voice she used as a child to ply me out of the darkroom. How much of her young life was spent waiting for me to emerge. If I add it up, what did I lose? A year. Two of hers? "You can't keep putting Dee off like this."

I make a face. I have no desire for an onslaught of heart-wrenching partings useful only to those who are staying on. A seeking of absolution if, for nothing else, the guilt they feel knowing they will outlive me. They should hold their good-byes until I'm actually gone.

"She's one of your oldest friends." Katie's voice that of a caretaker's. It shouldn't happen this early. When you're ninety a child can take over. Even then it's too soon.

"Mom, your friends need to talk with you." Her tone stern much like the one I used when she wouldn't stop interrupting me. "Friends need to see you. If one of them did that to you, you'd be furious."

"Too bad." I don't care if I'm behaving like a sullen four-year-old.

"Mom, let Dee come."

"So who's stopping her?" I sound like a Borscht Belt comedienne. I start to giggle. Katie does too. Then the giggle turns to a gasp. I inhale oxygen. "Okay. Tomorrow," I say.

"Do you mean it?" she asks? A single "yes" has never been enough for my daughter. I've seen that doubting expression from the time she learned adult promises might not be kept. When her father didn't send a present. Or didn't show. When I stayed out longer than intended. How did she survive us?

"Promise!" I say.

Kate races back to the phone. So, tomorrow begins the march of the goodbye-sayers. There will be those who come out of the woodwork. Acquaintances who will want the bragging rights to say they were included in the final days. And then the friends who wish to find comfort for their loss. Well, they shouldn't worry. Mourning a friend never lasts very long. In a few months they'll be seated in a coffee shop reconstructing my life as each think they knew it. It's what we did with Marianne. Marianne, the thief of my dilemmas. Berating me for anguishing over things that may never occur, only to take my turmoil and turn it into a wonderful piece of writing. But then, what is any story but a hypothetical situation turned into an author's reality?

We humans are ghouls. Declination and death should be private. The loss of self should not be imprinted on another's memory. The deterioration of our capacities not added to the sum of our lives, diminishing its total worth. How we scavenge through tales of dementia as if it were a huge dumpster. And what will they find? Not me. No matter what stories they tell, no matter what bits of trivia they gather, it won't be me. Only a fragmented self, partially assembled, colored by the prism of each individual eye.

My daughter re-enters victorious. Even now she is beautiful. Oh, not a classic beauty. But beautiful nonetheless.

"She's coming around lunchtime. I thought that best. I'll be here. And if you and Dee want time alone, I can become scarce."

I nod approval and watch as she trots off in search of more things to do. Next she'll start scrubbing walls.

What horrifies is the thought of friends issuing reports on my daily decline. Not as if I haven't been guilty of doing exactly that. . .

"Marianne peed in the bed."

"How awful."

"Right after she sipped the cappuccino I brought."

"You can't feel responsible."

"I know, but –"

"She told her sister she wanted to see George."

"You're kidding!"

"She couldn't have meant it. Do you think it was the meds? Maybe the cancer has hit her brain"

"Has anyone called him?"

"Lord no! Are you going over tomorrow?"

"Of course. You?"

"Haven't missed a day." . . .

It's what they'll do. It's what I did.

Strange how I always assumed I'd be found rotting on the floor with my dog whimpering by my side, both of us smelling to high heaven. Now I, too, will have nurses washing me down so the smell of death doesn't permeate the room. My child and lover will hover nearby. A friend or two will stand just outside, waiting to offer consolation.

"Katie?" She doesn't hear me. Shit. I don't like my own company today.

Tuesday, October 21, 12:35p.m.

I can hear Dee whispering. "How's she doing?"

Ask me, for God's sake. I'm still here. And I'm doing lousy, thank you.

Her voice takes on a bright overlay as she nears my door. "Katie you've got to show me pictures of the little one. She must be what, almost two?" They enter. My daughter first.

"Dee's here."

"I'm aware." I am also aware this is not how you greet an old friend. But, why not? She's alive and vibrant. And she's two years older than me. Not that she'd admit it. I only know her age, because once, when she was out of the room, I peeked in her purse at her driver's license, tired of her refusing to share her age when I was totally open about mine.

"It's about time you let me in, bitch," Dee says.

I have never gotten used to Dee's use of 'bitch' as a term of endearment. "Thought I'd spare you," I say.

"Death does not scare me, Darlin'. Besides, except for the oxygen, you don't look half as bad as I expected." There is a lightness in Dee's voice as if she really does enjoy death. Bet she wouldn't if she had to come with me.

Kate blanches. Death scares the shit out of her. Oh, Katie, I'm so sorry.

"Just promise me, Dee. No tears," I say.

"You're not going tomorrow. And I'll damn well cry if I feel like it."

"Not here you won't."

"Soph has put a moratorium on tears," Roger says as he enters. "How've you been Dee?"

"Fine if it weren't for this one doing something stupid like getting cancer. And as for you Soph, there's nothing wrong with crying. Cleanses the body."

"So does throwing up and I refuse to do that as well."

Katie shoves a chair closer to the sofa. Mischa, obviously thrilled with the possibility of a new playmate, jumps on it. Dee shoves him off and folds herself lotus style into the seat, so he jumps onto the sofa and curls himself around my feet.

"Can I get you a drink, Dee?" Roger asks.

"Hell, why not? Vodka. Straight up."

"You Kate?"

Kate shakes her head no.

"None for me?" I say.

Roger throws me a look.

"Just want to be asked." Kate stands stuck in conflict, anxious to protect me from what other truth Dee might put forth, and desperate to get away from hearing it. I give her a look to leave and she takes off for the kitchen.

"Busy little beaver, isn't she? So! How are you doing, Soph? Really."

I shrug. "Oxy-moronic. A part of me accepts it, the other finds it inconceivable." Dee's eyes bore in. "Probably no different for those waiting execution. To the end they must expect someone to call, 'Cut!'"

"Soph, don't make light."

"I'm not."

"Are you scared?" she asks.

"Do you remember my friend Caroline?"

"Vaguely."

"She kept popping pills until she could no longer make a simple sentence. On the other hand, Marianne—"

Dee cuts me off. "I knew you'd bring her up."

How could I not? Marianne, The Stalwart. The "I'll-do-it-myself" Marianne, reduced to a pathetic beggar, pleading with the nurses for more medication. And would they give it to her? Of course not. It could kill her.

"We are a barbaric society. If I want to put Mischa, young, vibrant, healthy Mischa, to death I can. But not a terminal human. Not me. That's what scares." Upon hearing his name, Mischa stands up, then realizing we're not ready to play lies back down.

"Do they know what you want?" Dee says motioning in the direction of the kitchen. I shake my head no.

"Why not?"

I shrug. I don't know what I want except a miracle. We sit in silence.

"Maybe I should get the goodbyes over with all at once," I say between breaths. "Throw a bash."

"Now that would be a fun event," her sarcasm evident.

"Seriously. A night filled with toasts. Zander could talk about my career. Maurice, what it was like to assist me. Janet, our late night phone calls."

"Janet has enough on her plate."

"You, the early days. Just delete intimate details. Roger doesn't need to know how many we bedded. Someone who spent thirty years with one person would never understand."

I love the image of Dee standing in my loft, in one of her long black baggy dresses with gobs of exotic jewelry draped around her neck and ears, her close-cropped hair accenting her bones, recounting some of our escapades. "You can tell who we met at what bar. Just not that we went home with most of them. I'll sit between Kate and my soon-to-be widower."

"You and Roger getting married?"

"No."

"I just thought when you said widower."

144

"A slip. He's Beth's widower. He'll be my mourning significant other? We've wrecked our language."

Silence.

"You know what really worries me?" I watch her spine straighten ever so slightly as if good posture will make whatever I have to say easier to handle.

"What?" she asks.

"Who I'll spend eternity with." Her body relaxes.

"Since when do you believe in an afterlife?"

"Since I have to leave this one. Roger will join Beth. Thirty years wins out over our measly two."

"Not necessarily."

"Right." I say sarcastically. But it does bother me.

"Well, you're Roger's last love which has to count for something."

"His latest. Not his last. Men can't be alone." I should make Roger promise if he is not going to be with me for eternity, then he damn well better be next to me as I die. Not out taking a walk. Or dozing off in the next room.

"Well, you won't be alone. I'm sure Marianne will enjoy the company. Soph?"

Here it comes. The protestation of undying friendship. The prelude to parting.

"I can't stand to think of you sitting around here waiting for the end."

Dee sure can surprise.

"Not just sitting." I tell her. "Archiving work. Getting ready for posterity."

"Which has to be depressing as hell."

"Never had the luxury of looking at work and not worrying about what's next."

"But you've finished, right?"

"Almost."

"What if you have six months instead of four?"

"It's three. Not that I've been counting."

"What if you have six? What would you be doing with them? You've thrived on work. So why stop now?"

4:30p.m. I must have dozed off. Mischa's sprawled over my legs. Katie's sitting in a chair across from the sofa looking at me. "Where's Dee?" I ask.

"She left ages ago.

"And Roger?"

"Went for a walk."

"Without Mischa?"

"Mom. . ." you can see her editing her thoughts. "He just needed to get some air. Translation: he needed to get away from all of this.

"You seem to know what he needs."

"Mom, I . . ." Another thought deletion.

"Katie, just so you know, I've told him more than once he doesn't have to live through this with me. He should get out. Leave."

"For Christ's sake, Mom. He wouldn't do that." She deletes: Who could live with the guilt? "It's just every so often he needs a break. . . He went to meet a friend for a drink."

"Male or female?"

"Christ!" Another deletion: You think he's having an affair? At his age. With you dying?

"Male or female?" I want an answer.

"I didn't ask. It's none of my business." Unsaid: Her mind is going.

But my mind is not going. At least as far as I know. Only sex is. Roger no longer desires me. Or haven't you noticed he now touches me only in the most medicinal way.

Wednesday, November 15, Morning

I used to argue with Marianne that writers and photographers were different breeds. That Marianne and her like need to immerse themselves in a whole gestalt in order to practice their craft. Whereas we visual artists–and I do consider photography an art no matter how it is currently practiced–create one perfect gestalt from a single image. Hear me now, Marianne. I do at last concede we were more alike than not. That we both feed selfishly on our experiences, knowing we can transform whatever horror we are living through into something beyond itself, with its own form, its own reality. Why else would I, who shuns the macabre, the maudlin, the easy photograph, be directing Katie to position cameras and lights around my room, so I can document my demise? In black and white, no less.

"What if I pull it back a bit? Away from the bed so you won't knock it over," she says.

I motion for Kate to leave the tripod as is. Words now kept to a minimum: energy conservation. She seems relieved not to have to move it again. Incredible how she can handle her child with extreme confidence, yet treats my equipment as if it were expensive crystal that will shatter under the slightest touch. Did I warn her away from it once too often? Or, was it her archrival, her sibling?

"I still don't like the idea of blacking out the room. It's unhealthy."

I toss her a visual "Oh really?"

"You know what I mean," she says.

At least she stopped tiptoeing around me. Put off any immediate concerns as to last-word regrets.

"Roger agrees with me, you know. He doesn't think you should spend twenty-four hours a day under floods any more than I do. Christ, you never allowed me to turn on a light, even to read by, until it got dark."

I want to say, "So that's the reason why you still don't need glasses," but it's another of the hundreds of thoughts a day unshared due to lack of breath. "Floods," I say. The dark something I am no longer comfortable with. Years spent in a dark room watching images flow up before me representing life itself. Now only bright lights feel safe. I get out "consistency of images." I sound like a rasping fog horn.

"Then let us use a light meter."

"No!" I croak. Too adamant. I mustn't alienate.

"I know how to use one, you know."

"Not the point." It isn't. I must extricate a deathbed promise from Zander not to exhibit anything I would not approve. But how will he know? How would anyone know exactly what I want? No. What's caught in the camera must be perfect. Ready to show. No corrections.

"Mom, where are you going?"

"Angle."

"It's exactly how you set it. No one's moved it."

I lurch forward. My legs move faster than my breath can carry them.

"Go slow for God's sake!"

I grab onto the tripod as Katie races to steady me.

"Damn it, Mother, can't this wait until Maurice gets here? He is your assistant for Christ's sake."

"Was."

"Was, is, what difference? He'll know exactly what you want."

Is she still jealous? "Be me." I order.

"M-o-m!"

Once again, she's the railing teenager trying to separate from me without a father to hold us together. I point for her to lie down on the bed with her head where mine would be.

"Me!"

"I'm not posing as you, Mom. You're asking too much."

I don't need her to pose. I just want to see her through the lens. The world there is so much clearer, one's focus unencumbered by extraneous matter. My son-in-law says it's how I retrieve the pixels of life. How did my daughter manage to pick so well on her first try? I make a motion for us to exchange places and sink down onto the bed.

"Focus!"

"I'm sure it's fine, Mom. If not, Maurice can check it."

"Focus!" I rasp.

She stands behind the camera uncomfortably dislocating her head from her body in order to fit her eye behind the lens. So this is what I looked like to her so much of the time. Poor child. Rarely saw her father, and her image of her mother was a partial face with a black box in front of an eye.

"Mom, let's take a break."

I search my daughter's face as if it were a mirror in which I could see just how frightful I must look. But she's become quite adept at camouflage.

"Besides, you've got to eat. What do you want for lunch?"

What do I want? I want to keep working. I want to see the finished product. I want her to promise she'll see this project through once I am no longer in control of my mental faculties. I want her to swear she's not humoring me. And I want to hold on to our every moment together while releasing her from all attempts to make each one meaningful.

"Whatever."

"Then rest a bit."

She turns to go and then looks back. To fix me in her mind? To assure herself I won't get up? I'd like to get up. Check the shot. Decide how I'll re-frame the shot once the morphine drip arrives. How I'll focus the lens. Should I be the ghost or let the paraphernalia hover like ghosts in the background. Specters that enhance but do not compete with the subject matter: The patient as a still life. Or should it be "Stilled Life?" Either one a good title.

I used to think Katie refused to develop her talent so she would not have to compete with me. But this was not the case. She knew, way before I was ready to conceive of the possibility, she had not inherited my eye. Oh, she learned to differentiate between the good, bad or simply mediocre, but she was never able to envision what was yet to be created.

I hate not being in control. Hate the thought of my former assistant taking over. Zander will tout the show as the final collaboration between the one-time protégé and his master. A strange expression: Master and protégé. Is the master a master of his work or of the protégé. And if of the work, does everything he produces automatically become a masterpiece? I should be ashamed of myself. Years of feminist indoctrination and I insert the male pronoun.

Obviously, I am not now, nor ever have been a true master. What master pushes a young disciple to go out on his own? Takes time away from her own work to set up his studio? Promotes his work to her dealer? A true master keeps servants indentured without qualm. When the studio burns, the true artist rescues the painting not the dog. I have no doubt I'd leave all my work engulfed in flames and grab Mischa. Though try and convince Katie of that. . .

"Is that what's bothering you? "Your relationship with Katie?"
"What?"
"Is that what's bothering you? Is Katie what's bothering you?"
"She says I put my work before everything, even her."
"Do you?"
"No, she comes first. I'm simply trying to set a good example. To instill in her respect for whatever she chooses to do. I refuse to let her think female artists are not as important as men. You know, doctor, it's not about talent, but selfishness. Men are simply better at that than we are."

Now that would make an interesting shot: Katie's arm reaching over just as the timer goes off as she arranges the sheets. Wrong. Too little contrast. Even if she wears a dark sweater, she always pushes the sleeves up way too far. I wish she had my addiction to black.

Maybe the camera will catch Roger sunk into the chair with his legs extended, feet crossed at the ankles, in his best Lincoln-esque pose. His long boney fingers sensually dangling. Marianne used to say a flaccid penis wasn't sexual. But then she never got to see Roger's fingers with their portent of things to come. He was a surprise. I'd always thought the relationship between digits and penis rather hit and miss. I could point the camera at the mirror and position the mirror to catch the scene. Then it could be "Reflections of a Stilled Life."

They're not my pictures. Where are mine? "Zander, where are mine? There? Walls too long. Too narrow. Not how to show my work. And the prints. Too small. Out of focus. People are going to laugh. They are laughing. Where's the door? Where have you put the door? Got to get out of here. Can't breathe. Get me out!"

150

"Soph? Soph! Wake up, Soph. Wake up!"

"Pictures. Wrong."

"You're drenched. What pictures?"

"Too small."

"Soph! Wake up. You've been dreaming. Wake up!"

"Can't breathe."

"It's okay, Soph. The oxygen plugs fell off. Breathe slowly. It'll pass."

I have no memory of a dream.

"Mom?"

"She's okay."

"Are you sure?"

Please, may the follicles on my body lie flat. I hate being afraid.

December 4

He's asleep. Stretched out in the chair, feet up on my bed, newspaper unfolded over his legs. Interesting, he was the first man in years who turned me on. What was it? It wasn't looks. At a certain age looks fade into the crags. His smile? He had, has the warmest, most engulfing smile. "Congratulations. It's a good show," he said. Followed by, "Can I get you a drink?" I responded with "Hate gallery wine, but you can buy me one later." I actually said that. Risked hearing, "My wife and I would be delighted," "or "My wife and I have to get home," or "I'm here with. . ." Took one look at his smile and threw all caution to the wind. No, it was more than the smile. It was his eyes. They've always been my dénouement. Playful, sexy, teasing eyes. And God, did we play. The celibate Sopher–sex for the sake of sex having become a bore–found herself in bed within a week. Sex! Someone should explain why I can't get sex out of my mind. Lying here waiting to die and I'm thinking about sex. Having sex. Having had sex. God I want Roger to crawl into bed with me. Not that I could do anything. Just want to feel a warm body next to me. Hell, we had sex when he wasn't feeling well. Right after he threw up from a lousy dinner. A bit of mouthwash, and we went at it. So why can't he close his eyes, climb in with me?

I keep asking what day it is. I'm not sure why it's so important to know. They tell me and then I can't remember and ask again. I must be driving them crazy. I can hear them vaguely. "Is Roger here?" "Walking Mischa." "It's almost over." "Shhh. She can hear you. Hearing the last thing to go." Loud noises. Rasping noises. Mine?

"I love you, Mom. I'll always love you," Katie says.

"Me you too."

"It's just ice, Mom. To wet your lips."

I shake my head, no. It's enough.

About the Author

Margo Krasne, born and raised in Manhattan, has always led two lives. As a radio advertising producer, she sculpted; as a sculptor, she was an extra in commercials; and for the past 24 years, as a communications coach and author of *Say It With Confidence*, she wrote fiction whenever possible—including a two act, two character play: *Attachment*. This is her first collection of stories.

CPSIA information can be obtained at www.ICGtesting.com
Printed in the USA
LVOW131239071112

306239LV00001B/336/P